What Are Friends For?

Mildred Ames **What Are Friends For?**

CHARLES SCRIBNER'S SONS
New York

Copyright © 1978 Mildred Ames

Library of Congress Cataloging in Publication Data
Ames, Mildred.
    What are friends for?
    SUMMARY: Eleven-year-old Amy finds that her
relationship with Michelle test all of her notions
about the true nature and responsibilities of
friendship.
    [1. Friendship—Fiction] I. Title.
PZ7.A5143Wh   [Fic]   78-13747
ISBN 0-684-15991-0

To the Warner girls, Alice and Peggy

What Are Friends For?

One

A Classic Case of Total Rejection

AMY SAT ON her bed, staring at her doll collection, wondering how to tell Michelle that she couldn't walk home from school with her the following day. Finally she said out loud, "You know, sometimes I think the only reason Michelle and I are best friends is because we're both divorced."

She often talked to her dolls. She could say things to them that she couldn't say to anyone else. In fact, they knew everything there was to know about Michelle right from that first day two months ago.

Amy was new to southern California then. She and her mother had moved into an apartment in Redondo Beach only the day before. In the late morning, while her mother was still unpacking, Amy walked up to the neighborhood deli to buy the makings for lunch. When she returned with her groceries, the elevator was in use. She pushed the button and waited. As she stood there, she looked down to find a Siamese cat sitting beside her, paying her no attention, looking as if he, too, was waiting for the elevator.

Amy had to smile. "Whose kitty are you?"

The cat glanced up, gave her a noncommittal stare, then as the elevator door automatically opened, walked into the car with all the nonchalance of a seasoned traveler.

"Oh, no, kitty." Amy hurried after. She quickly set down her groceries, pushed the button to hold the door open, then picked up the cat.

As she placed it outside, a voice said, "It's okay." Amy looked up to see a pudgy girl of about her own age, eleven, come bounding into the car. "That's Mousy Tongue," the girl said. "He lives on the fifth floor. He's Mrs. Lovelace's cat."

The cat took a moment to give Amy an indignant stare, then scurried back in beside her.

"Mousy Tongue—" Amy began to laugh. "What a funny name."

The girl never cracked a smile. Instead, she raised her eyes to the ceiling in a look that implored God to save her from all the imbeciles of the world, then pushed the fifth floor button.

When the elevator began to move, Amy ventured, "Fifth is my floor, too."

"I know. I saw you move in yesterday." Nothing about the girl's tone encouraged conversation.

They rode in silence, the girl staring fiercely ahead, Amy sizing her up out of the corner of an eye, not liking much of anything she saw: a great unruly bush of kinky blond hair, a sullen face almost swallowed up in huge aviator-style glasses, and behind them light blue eyes that glared at the door as if trying to stare it down. All of it added up to instant dislike.

Amy turned her attention back to the Siamese, who was now making good use of his time for a quick bath.

The silence lasted until they passed the second floor. Then the girl said, "That's not really his name."

Not expecting further conversation, Amy glanced up in surprise. "Huh?"

"Mousy Tongue—that's not really his name."

"Oh." Amy wasn't about to give this hostile girl the satisfaction of asking questions. Instead, she stared into her bag of groceries, pretending indifference.

In a moment, the girl said, "That's only what I call him. His name is really Mao Tse-tung. I thought you'd get it."

In spite of herself, Amy giggled. "That's funny."

The girl shrugged. "I don't know why Siamese cats always have to have Oriental names. It must be a law or something."

Amy smiled. "Does he always ride the elevator?"

"Oh, yes. Unless he can't find someone going up or down. Then he takes the stairs."

"What if someone's only going to the second floor?"

"Everybody here knows Mousy. They always push the fifth floor button for him."

As the elevator came to a stop, the cat sprang to the door and waited until it opened just wide enough to accommodate his slender body. Then he slipped through.

Amy laughed again. "That's so funny. I never knew a cat that could take an elevator." She stepped out of the car and watched Mousy head down the hall.

"I'm so used to him I don't think anything about it." The girl joined Amy and the elevator door closed behind her. "I guess you didn't see me yesterday."

"I guess I didn't."

"I saw you and your mother when you were moving in." She paused significantly. "I didn't see your father though."

Amy felt her lips tighten as she said, "He's in the East."

"On a business trip?"

"No." The last person Amy wanted to talk about was her father. "Not exactly."

"I guess it must have been hard, moving without your father's help—I mean, lifting and all."

Amy felt sure that the girl was prying. "It wasn't so bad."

"Well, that's just like a man—at least, that's what my mother always says. She says they only turn up when all the hard work is over. I'll bet that's what your father's doing—waiting until everything is done."

When Amy frowned but said nothing, the girl went on relentlessly. "He'll probably show up this weekend when you're all settled."

Why couldn't she let up? Amy had thought her tears long past, yet she felt her eyes sting now. She turned away. "I really have to go—"

Before she could hurry off, the girl said, "I thought so," in a voice so quiet she might have been talking to herself, a voice that compelled Amy to turn back in spite of the tears.

"Thought what?" Amy said.

"You're divorced."

The words pricked like an accusation. "I—I—"

"I can always tell. That's because I'm divorced, too. You know the saying—it takes one to know one."

Amy could feel the tension inside her ease a little. If this girl had shared the same experience, there was no reason to feel ashamed in front of her. "That's a funny way to put it. I mean, I never thought of it that way—*me* divorced."

"Well, if you look it up in the dictionary, you'll think of it that way. Actually, I guess I should say *we're* divorced—Hugo and I. He's my twin brother. I'm Michelle Mudd. And don't make any cracks about it, because I've heard them all."

"I'm Amy Warner—and I wasn't going to make any cracks."

"Okay." Michelle's tone said, I believe you but just

keep it in mind. Then her pale eyes rested thoughtfully on Amy for a moment. "Hey—you want me to show you the neighborhood? There's a neat occult shop in the village."

Amy had just returned from that local shopping center but she had noticed only the deli. "You mean the kind of shop that sells things for magic spells?"

"Something like that. I'll show you—this afternoon, if you want."

"I guess I *should* help my mother this afternoon."

"Okay, then—tomorrow."

Although, at first, Amy had had great reservations about Michelle, in the few weeks before school started, a friendship began to develop between the two. Amy decided that it was mostly because they were both divorced. You had to go through a divorce yourself to really understand someone else who had. Amy and Michelle compared experiences.

"At first," Michelle said, "I thought it was all my fault, y'know?"

"You did? That's *exactly* how I felt. Exactly!" Until now, Amy hadn't known exactly how she had felt. It took Michelle to put the feeling into words for her. Of course, Michelle had been divorced longer. For Amy, the time was still measured in months. "Did you ever get over that feeling?"

"Oh, sure. My dad's a psychiatrist. He's always telling me how I feel before I know it myself. Even if he's right, I tell him he's wrong. I don't want to turn into a classic case."

"What do you mean?"

"Oh, you know—like all divorced kids have to act a certain way. The 'divorced child syndrome,' my dad would call it. Makes you feel like a stereotype."

For Amy, Michelle was speaking a new language. "I guess I really don't understand those words."

Fortunately Michelle seemed to enjoy explaining. "It's like when you have measles, you have certain symptoms. Well, in psychiatry, you have syndromes. That's just a set of symptoms. I guess all divorced kids are supposed to have matched sets. My dad says to me," she mimicked her father's voice, "'Now, Michelle, you probably feel you are in some way to blame for your mother's and my divorce.' I say, 'No, I don't.' That shakes him up—he's expecting a classic. He says, 'You don't?' I say, 'No, I don't. I know who's to blame—Mom.' Then he goes through a big thing about how no one is to blame. I don't even bother to listen, because once I say it, I know I'm right. It *is* my mother's fault. She's got no loyalty. She just can't stick to one man. And you *know* no husband is going to put up with that." Michelle shook her head in disgust. Then she said to Amy, "How about you? Was it another man?"

"No."

"Another woman?"

Amy, not used to talking about it, nodded. Then she couldn't help saying, "And she has three children."

"Three children!"

"Uh huh. And I never want to see him or speak to him or have anything to do with him again."

9

"Well, that's natural." Michelle's was the voice of experience. "You have all the symptoms of a classic case of *total rejection.*"

Amy wasn't quite sure it was a good thing to have. And she remembered how Michelle felt about classic cases, so she said, "I'm not a classic case of anything. I'm just me, and that's how I feel. And nobody else can feel like me because they're not me. Besides, I don't want to talk about it anymore."

Of course, they did talk about it more. Much more. Partly because whether they walked on the beach or shopped, they spent a big part of every day together. By the time school began, they were fast friends.

When they were assigned to the same classroom, they were both delighted. Michelle said, "It'll be great to have someone to walk back and forth with now."

Amy asked, "How about your brother?"

"Oh, Hugo—he meets this kid he goes in with." There was a tinge of bitterness in Michelle's voice. "You know, once we used to be real close. Practically inseparable. We never even needed anyone else. Now he acts like I'm poison. He's just like my mother—no loyalty." Michelle scowled. "He might as well be like her. He's her favorite. Well, who needs him? Besides, I'd rather walk with you."

So each day they had walked to and from school and spent the afternoons together. And that was the trouble. "If I go to Barbara's house after school tomorrow," Amy said now, "how can I tell Michelle she can't come with me?"

She sighed. "I guess I'll just have to tell her the truth."

"Tell me *what?*" a voice said.

Amy whipped around to find Michelle standing in the bedroom doorway, frowning at her.

Two

A True Friend Would Have Understood

AMY'S MOTHER HAD answered the front door when Michelle knocked. Amy hadn't expected Michelle to come over so soon. Before Amy could collect her thoughts, her friend marched into the room and said, "I thought you didn't play with dolls anymore."

Amy flushed. "You know I don't *play* with dolls. I collect them."

"Well, you were talking to them. And you said you were going to tell me the truth. The truth about what?"

Amy hedged. "Oh, nothing—I was just talking to myself. Don't you ever talk to yourself?"

Michelle ignored the question. "I still want to know what you were going to tell me. What truth?"

Amy looked at the dolls that she had placed on a low cabinet facing the side of her bed. Silently she asked them, Shall I tell Michelle? They stared back reassuringly. No, I can't, Amy thought. Not yet. "The truth is—" She paused, trying to decide what the truth was. "The truth is I talk to my dolls. There! That's what I was going to tell you. Does that make me a crazy?"

Michelle rubbed her chin, then said, "Lie down."

"Huh?"

"I said, 'Lie down.'"

Amy had been sitting on the edge of her bed, facing the lineup of dolls. Puzzled, she stretched out on her back. Michelle pulled the desk chair over and sat down beside her. "Now, Ms. Warner," Michelle said, "tell me when you first began talking to your dolls."

Michelle planned to follow in her father's footsteps and loved playing psychiatrist, Amy knew. With mock seriousness, Amy said, "I have always talked to my dolls."

Michelle reached for a tissue on the night stand beside the bed, removed her glasses, wiped them vigorously, replaced them on her nose, focused them on Amy, and said, "Have your dolls ever talked back?"

Amy giggled. "Of course not."

"You may get up, Ms. Warner. You're not a crazy. A little neurotic, maybe, but not a crazy. That will be fifty dollars, please."

Laughing now, Amy got up from the bed. "Michelle, you're too much."

Michelle, straight-faced, said, "It's really nothing, madam." She dragged the chair across the room to replace it at the desk.

Amy very carefully picked up Mimi and returned her

to her spot beside the many other dolls in a secondhand display case. "Mimi's one of the most valuable dolls in my collection."

Michelle came over to peer through the glass window at the doll.

"She's a French Fashion doll," Amy told her. "They all have closed mouths and swivel heads."

"What's her face made of?"

"That's bisque. Her body is kid and her eyes are glass. Only the French knew how to make eyes like those. Some people call them paperweight eyes."

"How did you ever get started collecting dolls anyhow?"

"Through my great-grandmother Warner. She had a really priceless collection. She donated most of them to a museum before she died, but she kept a few for me. Mimi was one."

Michelle's eyes swept around the room, taking in Amy's collection, even the less valuable dolls that sat along open shelves. "How did you ever get so many?"

"Mostly they were gifts. When people know you collect something, that's all they give you for presents."

Although Michelle had often seen the collection, this was the first time she had shown anything you could call interest. The next thing Amy knew, Michelle had grabbed Gregor, a boy doll, from the shelves and was roughly examining him.

When Amy could stand it no longer, she said, "Please, Michelle," and took the doll from her friend's hands.

"He's one of my favorites." Although modern, he was already a collector's doll. Amy smoothed his Prince Valiant haircut and brushed a piece of lint from his turtleneck sweater before setting him down.

"Honestly," Michelle said, "you sure can make a big deal over owning a bunch of dolls."

Sounding a little self-righteous, Amy said, "You don't really own something like a valuable doll collection."

"What do you mean you don't own it?"

For once, Amy felt she knew something Michelle didn't. "You sound just like me when my great-grandmother gave me her dolls. I said, 'You mean they're mine now? I own them?' She said something I'll never forget. She said, 'Do parents own their children?' "

Michelle said impatiently, "Well, of course not."

Amy nodded. "That's what *I* said. She said the dolls really belonged in museums and that she was only leaving them in my keeping." It came back to Amy now that her great-grandmother had also said, "Treat them kindly and gently, as you would friends. Friends aren't people you own. They aren't even people you need. They're people you enjoy."

Michelle said, "The way I see it, if she gave them to you, they're yours. And *you* own them."

Michelle simply didn't understand. "Collecting dolls isn't just owning things. My great-grandmother said it was keeping a part of history in trust so that someday everyone could enjoy it."

"I'd never play trustee to any roomful of dolls."

The words cut sharply into Amy. She knew that Michelle had no real interest in the collection. Yet why couldn't she accept the fact that Amy had? Michelle was trying to put her down, Amy was sure, trying to make her feel the things she cared about were silly and worthless. And to think that only moments ago Amy had been so worried about hurting Michelle's feelings. Forget it! In a cool voice, she said, "After school tomorrow I'm going over to Barbara Delaney's house."

Michelle, looking perplexed, stared at Amy for a moment. Then she said, "You're going over to Barbara Delaney's house?"

"Uh huh. Tomorrow after school."

Michelle's forehead settled in angry wrinkles. "Why would anybody want to go over to *her* house?"

Regret immediately filled Amy. She never should have blurted out things that way. How could she have been so mean, thinking she would take satisfaction from hurting her best friend? And she *had* hurt Michelle. She could tell. What if Michelle never spoke to her again? That was the last thing Amy wanted. She said quickly, "It's only because her mother found an old doll in Barbara's grandmother's trunk. Her grandmother said Barbara could have it. I told Barbara if she'd let me see it, I'd show her my doll collection."

"Oh, a doll—" The wrinkles in Michelle's forehead smoothed. Her lips twisted in a smile as she shook her head disparagingly. "I might have known. Well, I'll go with you."

Now Amy *really* hated herself. She looked at Gregor instead of at Michelle as she said, "Barbara says her mother won't let her have more than one kid in the house after school."

"Oh." The word came out flat.

"But we'll come here right after I see the doll. You can come over when I show Barbara my collection."

"Oh, well—" Michelle shrugged. "Well, I guess not. I really don't want to see a doll anyhow. And I've already seen your collection. Besides, I have some shopping I've just got to get done tomorrow."

"Do it today. We're going to walk up to the village anyhow."

"Oh, didn't I tell you? I can't go out this afternoon. I have to clean my room."

Michelle clean anything? That was a lie and Amy knew it.

"Yeah," Michelle said, glancing at the watch she always wore, a gift from her father. "I guess I'd better get with it." Then she trudged across the room, looking as if her feet were too heavy for her. Stalling? Hoping Amy would change her mind? Amy felt a little sick. No doll could be worth the bad feelings running through her now. Michelle looked like a classic case of *total rejection*. And Amy, of all people, knew how that felt.

She also knew the importance that Michelle attached to loyalty and to friendship. Their friendship. As Michelle hesitated, Amy opened her mouth to say she had changed her mind, that if Michelle couldn't go to Barbara's, neither would she. Before she could get out the words, Michelle wheeled around and said, "If you want to know, I just happen to think that people who play with dolls have all the symptoms of a classic case of arrested infancy. If you don't know what that means, it means they're still babies." Then she turned on her heel and, in the next instant, was gone.

Amy sucked in a deep breath which she exhaled in an angry huff. Damn Michelle!

When the front door slammed, she said to Gregor, "I don't understand her. Why did she have to get mad at me for a little thing like that? All I wanted to do was see a doll. Is that so awful?"

Three

Did Sleeping Beauty Wear Glasses?

THE NEXT MORNING as Amy picked up her lunch bag from the counter, her mother asked, "Where's Michelle? She's usually pounding on the door by this time."

"I guess she's late." Amy couldn't bring herself to talk about Michelle. Although she kept telling herself she was not at fault, she still felt guilty about her friend. Now she said, "Mom, please keep the living room picked up today. This afternoon I'm going to bring a girl over to see my doll collection."

"What's wrong with the living room?"

"Nothing—now. But you put papers and magazines all over the place when you're working."

"No, I don't."

"Yes, you do."

"Amy, if this girl is coming to see your doll collection, she won't care about the living room."

"Yes, she will!"

"Oh, for Pete's sake! Why should I care what she cares?"

"Because *I* care. Besides, *I* cleaned it up. I *always* clean it up." Which was only partly true. Nevertheless, Amy's neatness and her mother's untidiness were often at odds.

"So I'm not the world's greatest housekeeper—" Sounding injured, her mother paused, as if waiting for Amy to deny the words. When Amy said nothing, she gave a tolerant sigh. "All right, Ms. Clean, the living room will be in perfect order to serve high tea to your friend the grand duchess."

"Oh, Mom—" Amy chided. "You don't have to be sarcastic." Amy often suspected that either her mother's sarcasm or her housekeeping had caused the divorce. Maybe both.

"Amy, sometimes I think you have no sense of humor."

Amy said glumly, "There's a difference between sarcasm and humor."

"Yes, there is. Thank you for reminding me."

"That's just what I mean—you're doing it again. You're being sarcastic."

"Oh, for Pete's—Amy, I'm just not up to this sort of thing in the morning. Try me again later in the day. Maybe we'll both be in better moods."

Amy realized she was overdoing things a little. It was

20

simply that she felt so off-key today. She mustered the grace to say, "I'm sorry."

"I'm sorry, too. There. Now we're friends again. Come kiss me good-bye."

Amy gave her mother a peck on the cheek. Before she could leave, her mother said, "I'm glad you've found a new friend, honey. I was beginning to get worried about you."

"Worried? Why?"

"At home you used to have so many friends. Since we've lived here you haven't had anyone but Michelle."

Amy was only too well aware of that fact today. Back in Connecticut, she'd had four really good friends. If you were mad at one, or even two of them, there were always the others. Amy still missed them. "The kids out here just don't seem friendly—not like they were at home."

"Oh, I'm sure that's not true. People are the same all over. Give it a little time."

But Amy *had* given it time. Two months, to be exact. Maybe Michelle was right. She had known most of the class from the previous year. "I always wind up with all the creeps," she'd complained. Maybe they weren't all creeps, but they certainly were strange. If you tried to act friendly with them, before you knew it, they were edging away as if you had something catching. Amy had no time to dwell on the subject because her mother said, "Hurry up now. You don't want to be late."

Outside the apartment, Amy stood at a loss, wondering

what to do about Michelle. She finally decided to knock on the Mudds' door. If Michelle was there, Amy would pretend there was nothing wrong. If Michelle had left, then Amy would know she had at least tried.

As she approached the Mudds' apartment, their door swung open and slammed shut as Hugo dashed out. Amy opened her mouth to ask about Michelle, but he raced past, flinging a curt "Hi" in her direction, and disappeared down the stairwell.

Amy closed her mouth and knocked on the door. In a moment, Michelle's mother appeared, a plastic cape about her shoulders, her silver-blond hair caught back with a wide makeup band, little pearl earrings dangling from pierced ears. It flashed through Amy's mind that something about the woman looked lopsided.

"Oh, Amy—" Mrs. Mudd sounded as if Amy's presence was one more irritation in a particularly irritating morning. "Well, don't stand there staring at me. Come in."

Amy hadn't realized that she was staring. As she stepped inside, it dawned on her why Mrs. Mudd looked lopsided. Only one of her false eyelashes was in place. "Is Michelle ready for school yet?"

"Michelle's not going to school today. She has the sniffles. Or so she says."

Michelle always complained that her mother favored Hugo. "He lies to her all the time," Michelle had said, "and she still believes him. Even when I tell the truth, she doesn't believe *me*."

Mrs. Mudd said, "I'm not writing any excuses for her unless she stays in bed all day. I had enough of her goofing off last year. I've warned her. If she keeps on, she can just go live with her father."

Michelle's mother was always threatening her with that fate. Michelle paid no attention, though. "That's just talk," she said.

Amy was secretly relieved at not having to face Michelle. Then a weak voice issued from the direction of her bedroom. "Who is it, Mom?"

Mrs. Mudd said, "You can go in for a minute, Amy. But don't get too close to her, just in case."

Not at all sure of how Michelle would greet her, Amy was tempted to say that she had to run or she'd be late for school. Then she thought, What if Michelle really *is* sick? As usual, her mother doesn't believe her. What if Michelle doesn't get any medicine and dies? Sometimes things like that happen. Then Amy would never forgive herself for dashing away.

She quickly made for Michelle's room. At the door, she peered inside, across the rubble of clothes, books, games, and—there was no other word for it—garbage that always cluttered the floor, and over to the bed where a wan Michelle lay buried to her chin, her hair a great kinky halo against the bed pillow. On the wall behind the bed, an Age of Aquarius poster loomed over her.

"Hi," Amy said.

Michelle's arm struggled out from under the covers to grope on the bedside table for her glasses. With seemingly great effort, she placed them on her nose and turned droopy eyes on Amy. "Oh, it's you."

Amy picked her way through the debris on the floor to the foot of the bed. "I'm sorry you're catching a cold."

"Is that what my mother told you?"

"She said you had the sniffles."

Michelle slumped down farther in the bed and drew the covers tight about her neck. "Yeah. Well, I didn't want to worry her."

"What do you mean?"

Michelle sighed. "Actually, I think I've probably got pneumonia."

"Pneumonia? Why pneumonia?"

Michelle's hand shot from under the covers to clutch her throat as a fit of coughing overtook her. When the bed stopped bouncing, she rasped, "It's all in my lungs," and patted her chest.

That seemed the wrong spot for lungs, Amy thought. "Maybe I'd better tell your mother what you think."

"No," Michelle said quickly and clearly. In another moment her voice was raspy again. "I wouldn't want to worry her. She has so much responsibility—two kids to bring up, the shop to run. Oh, no, I just couldn't burden her with my pneumonia."

Michelle had never worried about burdening her mother before. And she always acted as if her mother's dress shop ran itself. Amy was beginning to suspect that Mrs. Mudd was right. Michelle was faking. "I don't think you have pneumonia," she said.

Michelle's eyes darted to her. "Why not?"

"Because my great-grandmother had pneumonia and she couldn't even talk."

"Well, my case just hasn't advanced yet."

"My great-grandmother was awfully sick right away."

Michelle's eyes rested thoughtfully on Amy for a moment, then closed. She gave a pathetic little moan. "I'm afraid you're right. I wasn't going to tell you. Actually, I think I've got something a lot worse than pneumonia."

"What could be worse than pneumonia?"

"Actually, I'm afraid I have," she whispered the words, "sleeping sickness."

"Sleeping sickness!" Amy almost laughed out loud. "Nobody gets sleeping sickness anymore."

Michelle's eyes popped open. In an indignant voice, she said, "That's all you know! Don't you read the newspapers? It's in all the papers—how it's going around in this country—whole epidemics of it. *Epidemics!*"

Whatever Michelle had, Amy was sure it wasn't sleeping sickness. This had to be a plot of Michelle's to get Amy to rush to her sickbed instead of to Barbara's after school. "I've got to go," Amy said. "I'll be late."

"You know, with sleeping sickness, you can fall asleep for years."

Like Sleeping Beauty, Amy thought.

"Or sometimes you only sleep for a week or so, then you die. Either way, you *always* die."

"You'll probably be okay by tomorrow," Amy said.

"No, I won't! Not with sleeping sickness."

25

Now Amy didn't know what to say or do. "I guess I'd better go." She backed into a heap of dirty clothes.

"Wait a minute," Michelle said urgently. "Don't go yet. I've got something I think I should tell you."

"What?"

"Well, I wasn't going to say anything, but I think you should know."

"What?"

Michelle sat up and gave her attention to the bed-covers, folding the edges this way and that as she talked. "It's about Barbara Delaney."

Amy had expected a new disease. "What about her?"

"Well, you know how nice everybody thinks she is?"

Amy shrugged. "Most of the kids seem to like her."

"Oh, I know. I did, too—at first. I just thought she was really, really nice, y'know?" Michelle made careful pleats in the bedclothes. "There was this girl in school last year. Barbara was so sweet to her, just like she is to everybody. You know that gooey sweet voice she has. This girl had Barbara to her house one day, and the next day you know what Barbara said?"

"What?"

"She said that the girl had no manners. She called her a pig. And she said her house was dirty and her father was a drunk. And after telling everybody that, Barbara was still gooey nice to this girl's face. I mean, I don't know how you feel about people who are nice to your face, then talk about you behind your back, but I—"

"Who was the girl?"

"Nobody you know. I can't remember her name now. She moved. But she's not the only one. I could tell you stories about—but I guess I shouldn't say anything." Michelle shook her head sadly. "I really liked Barbara, y'know?"

If Michelle had an illness, Amy was sure it had to be jealousy. Now Michelle was even making up stories about Barbara. You had to feel sorry for Michelle, but you didn't have to give in to her. Or believe her. Amy said, "I really have to go now. I hope you feel better soon."

Michelle let out an anguished sigh, sank back into the pillows, and closed her eyes. "I may sleep for years and years."

Without a word, Amy picked her way to the door. Then she couldn't help glancing back. Michelle, still wearing her glasses, appeared to have fallen into her long, long sleep. Amy suddenly thought that the books never mentioned whether or not Sleeping Beauty wore glasses.

⚜Four

Two Against the World

BARBARA POINTED TO one of the old dolls in Amy's display case. "That one has a china face like my doll's."

"Except it's pink china. Yours is white," Amy said.

"Is pink better?"

As it turned out, Barbara's doll, although old, had the most common of china faces, white, and therefore the least valuable. Amy hadn't the heart to tell her, though. "I wouldn't exactly say pink was better—depends on which you like best."

"I guess I like white."

"Me, too," Amy lied.

Barbara's eyes lit on a baby doll. "Oh, isn't she dear," she said in a sweet, sweet voice, the same voice that Michelle had called gooey sweet.

It only proved how wrong and nasty and vicious Michelle could be. Barbara, in her sweet, sweet voice, had, quite properly, drooled over each doll Amy had pointed out and had, quite properly, expressed admiration for Amy's considerable doll knowledge. In spite of anything Michelle thought, Barbara was really nice, Amy decided. She beamed now like a proud parent. "That's a 'Bye-Lo Baby.' Grace Storey Putnam, the woman who designed her, made her look just like a four-day-old infant."

"She's so darling. Could I hold her?"

Amy hesitated for only the briefest moment. Then she said, "Sure. But be careful. She's pretty old. She dates back to the 1920s."

"Oh, I'll be careful."

Amy took the Bye-Lo Baby from the case and placed it trustingly in Barbara's arms. After all, Barbara, unlike some people, knew how to appreciate valuable collector's items.

Like a little mother, Barbara cuddled the doll. In fact, Amy decided, that was exactly what Barbara, a very small girl, reminded her of. A little mother. She was always straightening someone's collar or picking stray bits of lint off someone's clothes or giving someone's cheek a comforting pat.

With a smile as sweet as her sweet, sweet voice, Barbara looked at the Bye-Lo Baby. "She is so so dear. I just love her." She turned the same smile on Amy. "I don't know how you ever learned so much about dolls and dollmakers and everything."

"Mostly from library books. When you're really interested in something, you can learn a lot from books."

"I don't know. I don't think I'd ever remember all those facts."

Amy felt pleased with herself. And generous. "Oh, sure you would—if you'd been at it as long as I have."

Barbara, her arms full, nodded toward the group of tiny wood dolls in the display case. "What are those?"

"They're called 'Penny Woodens.' That's because they sold for a penny in the olden times. They were my great-grandmother's."

"They're cute. What's the doll with the wrinkled face and the basket in front of her?"

"That's Annie, my peddler doll. Her head is made out of an apple."

"An apple!"

"Uh huh. They use a fresh apple and it dries into all those wrinkles."

"What's in her basket?"

"Mostly things to sew with—needles and buttons and hooks and eyes. The tiny milk-glass bottles have herbs in them. The real peddler women used to sell cures to heal people."

The little doll in red cape and black hood smiled at them with a toothless mouth, looking pleasant and witchy at the same time.

"Honestly, I'm really impressed." Barbara glanced around the room. "I never saw a collection of dolls before except in our library." She went over to the bed, placed the Bye-Lo Baby down, and sat beside it. As she straightened the doll's dress, she said, "You know, Hisa Nakata really should see your doll collection. She still has all her old dolls. She'd be crazy about it."

"Really?"

"Janie Ball, too. She'd love to see it."

"You think so?"

"Oh, I know so." Barbara spoke with solemn conviction.

Of all the girls in her room, Barbara, Janie, and Hisa were the ones whom Amy most wanted to know. They always seemed to be a part of everything that went on. Even though she had Michelle for a friend, somehow Amy still felt left out of things. And a little lonely. In this new school, she'd even had the disturbing feeling that no one wanted to know her. Sometimes she wondered if it had something to do with the divorce, if everyone could look at her and see *Reject!* stamped all over her.

It had never occurred to her that her doll collection could serve as a means to make new friends. Now it seemed like just the right idea. But what would Michelle think? Amy pondered for a moment, then decided that whatever she thought, Michelle would get over it. After all, in spite of all Amy's fears, Michelle was still speaking to her. Amy said, "Maybe you could all come over tomorrow. I'll ask my mom to get some cake or something. If Michelle feels better, I'll ask her over, too, and we'll make a party out of it."

"Oh, Michelle—" Barbara said with distaste. "Well, I

don't know if Hisa and Janie would come if she came."

"Why not?"

Barbara played with the ribbons on the Bye-Lo Baby's bonnet. "I don't think they like her very much."

Amy remembered her own feelings about Michelle that first day—instant dislike. "That's because they don't really know her."

Barbara said matter-of-factly, "Nobody wants to."

That annoyed Amy. "But it's not fair. How can people say they don't like somebody when they don't even know her well enough to know whether they like her or not?"

Barbara seemed to be at a loss now. She untied the bonnet ribbons and retied them. Finally she said, "I know Michelle is your friend, so I don't really think I should say anything about her."

Now Amy was not only annoyed but curious. "Say what?"

"Well, nothing—only if you hang around with her, no one will ever make friends with you. They'll think you're like—well, like her."

Amy stared at Barbara, then flung herself into her boudoir chair and let out an angry gasp. "That is the most—" she could think of nothing bad enough, "the most unfair thing I have ever heard in my whole life." Now Amy understood why she was making no new friends in school. And she could hardly believe it. "You mean, because all the kids think they don't like Michelle, they don't like me either? Oh, that's prejudice. That is pure prejudice!"

Barbara looked a little upset now. "I didn't mean it that way exactly."

"Well, what way did you mean it exactly?"

Barbara went back to playing with bonnet ribbons. "I just meant I thought you ought to know. I mean, everybody thinks you're okay but—I mean—well, my mother says Michelle isn't a fit companion. Hisa and Janie's mothers won't let them hang around with her either."

Prejudice. Pure prejudice. Sure, Michelle put people off at first. Even Amy had felt that way. But when you knew her better, you found out Michelle had plenty of good qualities. She was generous. And loyal. And—well, a lot of other things that Amy couldn't quite bring to mind at that moment. "Mothers don't know everything. They certainly don't know Michelle."

"No, but I think they know something *about* her."

"Like what?"

"I don't know exactly. Something happened last year. Michelle and this girl in school who moved away were pretty friendly. Then something happened and this girl-who-moved-away's mother told somebody else's mother. Then everybody's mother found out."

"Found out what?"

"I told you—I don't know. My mother said she wasn't going to talk about it because she didn't want me spreading tales."

What kind of tales could anyone spread about Michelle? Amy wondered. Michelle never did anything really bad, nothing that other kids didn't do. Amy's mind immediately darted to her own most sensitive spot. One thing made Michelle different from some of the other kids—the same thing that made Amy different. Michelle was divorced.

The thought brought back Hanover Park, where Amy had lived until recently. And where no one was divorced. Certainly not Kathy Merrill, whom Amy had known all her life. After the divorce, Kathy could no longer come over to Amy's house or spend time with her. She was pointedly busy elsewhere.

It was true that the Merrills had always been strange people, narrow minded and fanatical. It was also true, as her mother pointed out, that Hanover Park—with its conservative heritage and the private roads that kept it isolated and insulated—was not the whole world. All the same, people like that made you feel diseased.

Now Amy felt sick. Barbara's mother had said Michelle was not a fit companion. That sounded, to Amy, like the Merrill treatment all over again. And Amy was not about to stand for that. It was not only a matter of loyalty to Michelle but of loyalty to herself.

Amy decided to test her theory. "Does your father think you shouldn't hang around with Michelle, too?" she asked Barbara.

"My father? I don't think my mother even told him."

"How about Hisa and Janie's fathers?"

Barbara shrugged. "I don't know about them."

Not one divorce in the bunch. Now Amy was sure that her suspicions were right.

Barbara was again tying and untying ribbons. "Maybe you could have Hisa and Janie and me over when Michelle isn't around."

It took everything Amy had to contain her bitterness. She made her voice as gooey sweet as Barbara's. "I really couldn't." Then she threw Barbara's words back at her. "My mother won't let me have more than one kid in the house after school. Naturally, I have to have my best friend, Michelle." Then Amy very deliberately got up from her chair and walked over to the bed. "And you really shouldn't play with those ribbons so much. They're very old. They might rip." She picked up the Bye-Lo Baby, set it back in the case, returned to the bed, gave Barbara a comforting motherly pat on the cheek, and said, "You understand."

Michelle, still in pajamas, opened the door only as wide as the safety chain allowed and peered at Amy. Although Michelle wore her usual frown, Amy had the feeling she was pleased to see her.

"Oh, it's you," Michelle said in much the same tone she had used that morning. "You know, in my condition, I shouldn't even be out of bed to answer the door."

"Then why *are* you?"

Michelle scowled. "Because my stupid brother couldn't stay home with me even for one afternoon, and I thought it just might be something important."

"It is important. I've got something I've just got to tell you right now."

A look of interest passed over Michelle's face. "Well, maybe you'd better come in." She unfastened the chain for Amy, then refastened it behind her. "I guess I'd better get back into bed before I catch a chill. With what I've got, chills are fatal, you know."

Amy followed as Michelle's great furry bedroom slippers, like dirty pink dust mops, scuffed through the house, heading for her bedroom. Inside, she made right for the bed, kicked off the slippers, and crawled under the covers.

Amy, usually repelled by the sight of the messy room, was too full of indignation now to give it a thought. She knew only that she would explode if she didn't speak her mind. And fast. She perched on the edge of the bed, opened her mouth to begin, then noticed Michelle's lips. Purple. "What's wrong with your mouth?"

"Huh?"

"Your mouth."

Michelle stared at Amy, her eyes blank. Then she opened the drawer of her night stand and rummaged through the jumble inside to pull out a mirror. She examined herself in it with clinical interest. "I see what you mean." She nodded thoughtfully. "I guess I'm starting to turn."

"What do you mean—turn?"

Michelle tossed the mirror on the bed, snuggled under

the covers, and sighed. "It's one of the symptoms of the disease. You turn blue."

For a moment, Amy's eyes fixed on the purple lips in horror. Then she noticed brownish smears at the corners of Michelle's mouth. Peanut-butter brown. She might have known. But that was beside the point right now. Right now, the point was that she had the magic words to cure Michelle's dread disease and couldn't wait to get them out. "You know, you were right," she said.

"Huh? What do you mean?"

"I mean you were right. Absolutely right."

"About what?"

"About Barbara."

"I was?"

"Yes, you were. You really had her pegged."

"I did?" Michelle propped herself up on her elbows, obviously curious now.

"Yes, you did. You said Barbara talked behind people's backs, and you were right. Absolutely right. She does. And you know what *that* is—that's two-faced. Ooooh, how I hate two-faced people!"

"Yeah, well, I told you." Michelle's voice held a touch of sympathy. "You can't trust people like—" she broke off. In the next moment, she peered at Amy, her eyes wary. "Who'd she talk about?"

"Who?" After Barbara had left, Amy, caught up in her moral outrage, had marched right to Michelle's apartment, taking no time to anticipate a question like that.

"Well—well, she—well, just everybody. She talked about everybody."

Michelle said cautiously, "Everybody? Me, too?"

Amy gave a little forced laugh. "Did I say everybody? I didn't really mean everybody. I meant—well, practically everybody." To avoid looking at Michelle, she pulled at a loose thread on the bedspread. "I guess you were the only one she didn't talk about. I guess she was so busy talking about everybody else that she just didn't get around to you."

"Oh." Michelle sank back into the pillows. "Well, I told you," she said again. "I'll bet I can guess who she talked the most about—Janie and Hisa."

"Well, yes—some," Amy said truthfully.

"I knew it. They're supposed to be her best friends. Ha! What did she say?"

"Well, she said—" Amy stopped herself. Naturally she couldn't go into what Barbara had said about Janie and Hisa without going into what Barbara had said about Michelle. "I really don't think I should say. If I did, I'd be doing just what Barbara does. And you know how we both feel about that."

Michelle's mouth hung open for a moment. Then she closed it, swallowed, and said, "Yeah."

Saved by her own quick thinking, Amy immediately changed the subject. "You were right about something else, too. We've got all the creeps in our room. And, what's more, I don't want to have anything to do with any of them!" The words made her feel virtuous and fierce and brave. She and Michelle would be two against the world.

"Yeah, well, I told you."

"You sure did." Amy glowered into space. After a moment, she said, "I sure wish you were going to school tomorrow."

Michelle was speechless for an unusually long moment. Then she sat up, plumped the pillow behind her back, leaned against it, and said, "Didn't I tell you? With this disease, when you start turning blue, you've reached the crisis."

"You have?"

"Oh, yes. Blue is the turning point. The danger has passed. After blue, patients are up and about the next day."

𝕱ive

Hair, Fingernail Clippings, and Mind Power

AMY COULD HEAR the sound of her mother's typewriter in the bedroom. As she made for the room, she kept thinking of what had happened in school that day. When Michelle wasn't around, Hisa and Janie had approached Amy. Hisa said, "Barbara told us that you've got all kinds of wonderful dolls."

Amy said cooly, "Well, not *all* kinds, but I do have a lot—kachinas and corncobs and Kabuki warriors, of course. And I have quite a few antique dolls—a lot of them foreign—and, then, some modern dolls. My most valuable modern is Jackie Kennedy." She felt gratified to see Hisa's eyes bug out, so she added, "They only sold five hundred Jackie Kennedys. She's a limited edition."

Hisa said, "Oh, I'd really love to see her. I'd love to see all your dolls."

Janie said, "Me, too."

Amy had looked down her nose as she said, "Right

now, I show them by invitation only. But if I ever open my collection to the general public, which I doubt very much, then even you will be welcome."

Now at her mother's door, instead of feeling pleased with herself, she felt disturbed. Her mother was staring into space, murmuring, "Irresistibly French. . . ." She paused over her typewriter, shook her head, waved her hand as if erasing the words, thought a moment, muttered, "Capture her heart with fragrance," considered that, nodded, then began to type.

"Mom," Amy said.

"Hmmm?"

"Michelle and I are walking up to the village. You want anything?"

Her mother stopped typing, stared at words on the paper, and said, "The incomparable Chanel."

"What's that?"

Her mother glanced up. "What did you say?"

Amy sighed and again asked if her mother wanted anything from the village.

"You'd better pick up some toothpaste. We're all out." Her mother got up, fished in a drawer for her purse, opened it, and absently handed Amy a bill.

"Mint or plain?" Amy asked.

Her mother stared right through her. In a dreamy voice, she said, "A blend of East and West, past and present."

Amy sighed again and left. Sometimes she wondered if

41

her mother's work had caused the divorce. When she was creating, her mother never seemed to belong to the world of people. Amy worried the thought for a moment, then pushed it to a corner at the back of her mind, a dark corner where she stored all her speculations on the divorce. One day, when enough were crammed in there, she would pull them out, examine them in the light, one against the other, and perhaps she would have the answer.

Now she hurried to the Mudds' apartment, collected Michelle, and walked to the village with her.

"Let's go to The Sorcerer's Den first," Michelle said. "They've got a book I want."

Amy was agreeable. Although the occult shop never held quite the fascination for her that it did for Michelle, she still found it intriguing. She liked the sweet smell of incense that always hung heavily about the place and the fat white candle that burned constantly as a symbol of the soul. More frightening were apothecary jars full of strange herbs. One of them was mandrake root, which Michelle assured her grew only under a hangman's noose. It was a shop that could stir the imagination and send exquisite shivers up the spine.

Michelle made right for the racks of paperbacks. Her father gave her a handsome allowance, so she always had plenty of money to spend. Amy poked about, taking in the unusual items on shelves and in display cases. A gleaming crystal ball that sat on black velvet attracted her until she learned the price. A hundred dollars, for goodness' sake!

When she felt that she had seen everything, she looked around for Michelle and spotted her in the jewelry corner, a couple of paperbacks tucked under one arm. As Michelle slipped a pair of earrings off a rack, Amy came up behind her and said, "You can't wear those. They're for pierced ears."

Michelle whipped around, a startled look in her eyes. In the next moment, her face relaxed. "You didn't have to sneak up behind my back and scare me half to death."

That was the last thing Amy had intended. "I wasn't sneaking," she said. "If I scared you, I'm sorry."

"Oh, it's all right. Forget it." Michelle glanced down at the earrings in her hand.

"Oh, how darling," Amy said. Two little glass balls, tiny versions of the crystal ball that Amy had admired minutes earlier, hung from gold chains.

"I was just trying to see if you could use them for divination."

"What's that?"

"You know—like you use big crystal balls—to look into the future. These are too small, though." Michelle put them back on the rack.

Amy stared at them, enchanted. She could visualize them swinging from her own ears. "You know, maybe we should get our ears pierced."

Michelle's free hand shot to an earlobe. She looked horrified. "That is the silliest, stupidest thing I ever heard!"

Amy was taken aback. "Why is it stupid? Lots of people get their ears pierced. My great-grandmother had her ears pierced when she was eight years old."

"Well, it's just stupid, that's all. Besides, my mother won't let me."

But Michelle's mother had pierced ears herself. Amy had often admired her earrings. "Did you ever ask her?"

"Well—well, sure."

"I don't think my mother would mind as long as I had it done by a doctor. Maybe if we had it done by a doctor, your mother would let you."

"No, she wouldn't!" Michelle turned away. Without another word, she headed for the counter with her paperbacks.

She was scared, Amy decided. Afraid of needles probably. Amy wasn't terribly fond of needles herself. Yet it seemed like such a good idea. Especially if they could have it done together and give each other courage. Well, so much for good ideas.

After Michelle paid for her books, they headed for the drugstore. Amy was standing in line at the counter, waiting to buy toothpaste, when she saw that Michelle had again found an earring display. This time she was examining great golden hoops, also for pierced ears. Amy smiled to herself. At least she had planted the idea. Maybe Michelle would change her mind.

Amy paid for her toothpaste, and they left for home. She noticed Michelle had bought a book on witchcraft, another on the black arts. The last thing Amy'd known,

Michelle was into fortune telling. "How come you're interested in witchcraft now?" Amy asked.

Michelle snapped, "How come *you're* interested in dolls?"

Amy bristled. Too often lately, it seemed, Michelle got in some little jab about the dolls. "I only asked a simple question," she said, not bothering to hide her annoyance.

"Well, you don't have to get mad. That just happens to be the kind of simple question there isn't any simple answer for. In the first place, I'll bet you don't even know what witchcraft is."

"Sure I do."

"What?"

Amy thought it over, then said, "It's learning how to cast spells and do bad things to people."

"That's black witchcraft. There's white, too, you know. If you learn how to cast spells for good causes, that's white. There's nothing wrong with white."

Amy shrugged. "I don't believe in that stuff anyhow."

Now Michelle was obviously annoyed. "That's all you know. Anybody who knew anything about witchcraft wouldn't say a thing like that."

"What am I supposed to know?"

Michelle let out an exasperated sigh. "Witchcraft just happens to be a way of learning how to focus your mind power. If you ever talked to a psychiatrist like my father, you'd find out just how powerful the mind is. It can even make you sick."

"What's that got to do with witchcraft?"

45

"I got it figured out that if you can do things to yourself with mind power, you can do them to other people, too. You just have to start focusing your mind in the right way."

"What do you want to do to other people? Make them sick?" Amy felt a little sick herself now.

"Of course not."

"Then what? And who?"

Michelle regarded Amy doubtfully. After a moment she said, "Well, I wasn't going to say anything, but I guess you, of all people, ought to understand."

"Understand what?"

"Well, my dad has a new girl friend. I think it's serious. I figure if I can learn to focus my mind power, I can make her disappear."

Michelle was right. Of all people, Amy could understand that. Now she was in complete sympathy. "Oh, I know just how you feel. I'd hate to see what happened to me happen to you. But how can something like that work? I mean, what can you do about it?"

"I don't exactly know yet. But I'm sure going to find out. I do know this, though. It helps if you can get something that belongs to the person."

"Like what?"

"Like hair or fingernail clippings—things like that."

That gave Amy the shivers. "If you could make her disappear, where would you make her disappear to?"

Michelle spent a moment mulling over the question.

When she spoke, she might have been talking to herself. "To another planet maybe . . . or maybe I'd make her disappear into thin air . . . or maybe into some nice dark grave."

"Oh, Michelle!" Amy was really horrified now.

"Well, I—well, don't you—" Michelle broke off, took one look at the expression in Amy's eyes, then began again. "Can't you even tell when somebody's kidding? I just meant I wanted to make her disappear, well, out of my father's life."

"Oh." The thought of hair and fingernail clippings and mind power made Amy feel uneasy. "Isn't that black witchcraft?"

"Of course not," Michelle said indignantly. "It's in a good cause, isn't it?"

Six

An Unexpected Gift

MOUSY TONGUE RODE the elevator with Amy and Michelle. At the fifth floor, he sedately went his own way while they made for Amy's apartment. Inside the door, the steady clacking of the typewriter greeted them.

"Your mother's really working hard," Michelle said.

"Mmmm," Amy said. "She's blending East and West and past and present."

"Huh?"

"That's the kind of stuff she writes about perfume."

Michelle's eyes made a complete circle. "Oh, wow."

"Hey, look." Amy pointed to a box in brown paper wrappings that sat on the entry table. "Oh, I bet it's from Betsy. She said she'd send me something." All excited now, she dashed for the parcel, picked it up, and shook it.

"Who's Betsy?"

"You know—my grandmother—the one who lives in New York who's on a world cruise."

"Oh, yeah."

Amy, about to rip off the paper, took one look at the label and stopped short. "Oh," she said, her voice falling.

"Oh, what?"

Amy frowned at the package. "It's from my father."

"Well, open it."

"I don't want anything from *him*."

Michelle shook her head disgustedly. "That is the stupidest thing I ever heard. You should take everything you can get and ask for more. That's what I do."

"But I'm not you—I'm me."

"Now, look—the way I see it, he wanted the divorce. Right?"

"Uh huh."

"Then make him pay for it—pay through the teeth!"

Amy stood there staring at the box, as a disturbing mixture of emotions, not the least of which was curiosity, churned inside her. "He already pays child support."

"Crumbs! Child support is just crumbs. Fathers owe their kids more than crumbs. Did you ever stop to think of that?"

"Well, yes," Amy said meekly.

"The way I figure it, if I can get enough stuff out of my dad—really expensive stuff—maybe I can keep him broke."

Amy glanced at her, perplexed.

"Don't you get it? If he's broke, who'd want to marry him?"

49

Amy never would have thought of anything like that. Even if she *had* thought of it, what would it matter? Her father had already remarried. And she never could have brought herself to ask him for anything anyhow. But, of course, she hadn't asked for whatever was in the package. And if you stopped to consider for a moment, which she did, Michelle was right. Fathers certainly owed their kids more than crumbs. She handed the box to Michelle. "Maybe you'd better open it. Be real careful though. Don't rip anything. I may do it up again and send it back."

It took forever to ease the string off the brown paper. Michelle grew impatient and wanted to cut it, but Amy was insistent. If she returned the gift, there must be no telltale mark to suggest that she had even peeked.

Finally Michelle had the package open, its wrappings removed intact. She lifted the lid off a white box, pulled out cardboard and excelsior, took one look at the gift, clucked her tongue, rolled her eyes, and said, "Just what you need."

"What is it?"

Michelle pulled out a doll, a note pinned to its dress. As if hypnotized, Amy moved closer. Michelle unpinned the note and handed it to her. Amy recognized her father's big scrawl.

The minute I found her, I thought of you—the same long brown hair and big brown eyes. Then I saw her name, Aimee. I knew she had to belong to you.

She's not a new doll, honey, but a doll collector, like yourself, won't mind that.

Hope you like her.

I love you,
Dad

No mention of the divorce. No reprimand for her refusal to see him or even speak to him on the phone. In an odd way, Amy almost felt cheated. She took another look at her father's gift, a beautiful young-woman doll wearing a Chinese dress.

"What did he say?" Michelle asked.

"He says she made him think of me."

Michelle cocked her head and examined the doll more closely. "Well, her hair's about the same color, and it's long and straight. And she's got the same color eyes. She's even got a tan like you."

"And that's all she's got like me. Except her name. And that's not even spelled like mine."

Michelle's eyes traveled from the doll to Amy and back to the doll. "I'd say there was a slight resemblance."

Scrawny Amy with her long thin face and her snub of a nose resemble the beautiful Aimee? "Oh, that's silly—I don't look anything like that."

Michelle made another quick appraisal. "Well, anyhow, you'll probably look like that when you're a teenager." She handed the doll to Amy.

Amy immediately returned it to the box. "I guess I'll send it back."

"And have him give it to one of *her* kids?"

Amy hadn't thought about *her* kids. One, she knew, was a girl younger than herself, probably just the right age for dolls. "Well, I just may keep it. Maybe I can trade it to another doll collector for something else."

"You don't know another doll collector."

"No, but I'll find one."

"I bet you don't. I bet you keep it."

"Why would you bet something like that?"

Michelle shrugged. "I don't know—just a feeling I have. Did I ever tell you about these psychic feelings I get?"

No, Michelle never had. But she made up for it now. She told Amy, at some length, all about her psychic feelings. When she finished, she said, "And that's the way it is every time. All of a sudden something washes over me like a giant ocean wave. I mean, it's so strong it almost knocks me down. In fact—" she paused. Her eyes glazed over and fluttered around as if they were loose in her head. "It's coming on right now—a giant wave." She closed her eyes, grasped her head between her hands, and swayed back and forth.

Amy grabbed Michelle's arm. "What is it?"

In an eerie voice, Michelle said, "It's coming clear now. I see us someplace with a lot of other people. Everybody's eating. Eating like crazy. I see ice cream, tons and tons of ice cream. And it keeps coming." She clutched her throat. "I can't breathe—I'm drowning—buried under ice cream—tons and tons of chocolate, strawberry, vanilla, butter pecan."

All through chocolate, strawberry, and vanilla, Amy stood open mouthed. At butter pecan, she came to herself. Obviously Michelle was only putting on an act. "Okay, you phony," she said, "where are we supposed to be?"

Michelle opened her eyes. In the next instant, she began to laugh uproariously. "Don't you get it? We're in Farrell's."

"How could I get it? I've never been to Farrell's."

Michelle looked shocked. "You've never been to Farrell's? I don't believe it!"

Which made Amy feel she was suffering from some gigantic gap in her education. "What's so special about Farrell's? It's just an ice-cream place, isn't it?"

"Just an ice-cream place! You gotta be kidding! Why, this place—this place—" Apparently the description defied words, because Michelle said, "I'm not even going to tell you—anyhow, you'll see for yourself."

"What do you mean?"

"I mean, you and I are going there next Friday."

"How come?"

"It's my birthday—Hugo's, too. My dad said he'd take us there if that was where we wanted to go. I don't care whether Hugo wants to or not. I said that I wanted to go but only if you could come, too. After all, you're my best friend, aren't you? Oh, yeah, I forgot to tell you. He's bringing his girl friend."

Michelle didn't sound at all irritated. Which surprised Amy. "Aren't you mad?"

"Of course not, silly. This will give me a chance to put the whammy on her."

"Oh, Michelle! You wouldn't—not at your own birthday party. You'd spoil everything."

"Relax. I'm not going to do anything there. I'll decide what to do later."

Amy felt relieved. In spite of her skepticism about Michelle's ability to perform magic, she'd had visions of the woman's disappearing before their eyes, maybe under all those tons and tons of ice cream that had buried Michelle seconds earlier.

The vision vanished as Michelle said, "Come on, now—you've got to help me think up a birthday present to ask him for. What's the most expensive thing you can think of?"

Amy pondered, then said jokingly, "A mink coat."

Michelle, perfectly serious, replied, "Hmmmm—I wonder." Then she shook her head. "No, my mother would talk him out of it. She says in a place like California, fur coats are vulgar. No, it's got to be something else. What about a color TV for my room?"

"*That* sounds pretty expensive."

"Good. That's what I'll ask for." Michelle grinned. "A big one. After all, my eyesight's pretty bad, you know."

That night Amy argued with her mother. Amy must call her father and thank him for the doll, her mother insisted. *No!* Well, at least, she must write a thank-you note. *No!* Amy was acting childish. So? At the very least, it was only civilized to thank someone for a gift. In the end, the bitter end, Amy finally agreed to the note.

She sat down in her bedroom and wrote:

Dear Mr. J. T. Warner,
   Thank you for the package. I did not open it. I cannot afford to send it back on the child support I get, which is really crumbs. I will give it to the needy.

Yours truly,
Amy Margaret Warner

Then she sealed and addressed the envelope. When her mother asked what she had written, she said, "I did what you said—I thanked him." Now Amy was acting mature. And civilized.

Before she went to bed, she couldn't resist another look at the doll. She took it out of the box and sat it on the cabinet with the dolls she had put there earlier. She studied it with a practiced eye. It was a good collector's doll, there was no doubt about that. She should be able to trade it for something interesting. Another modern, of course.

When she finally turned out her bedside lamp, her head was too full of distressing thoughts to go to sleep. She pushed them out by concentrating on dolls, every collector's doll she could bring to mind, dolls she had seen pictured only in books, dolls she might someday own: Shirley Temple, Scarlett O'Hara, Cinderella, Peter Pan, the Lone Ranger, and even a doll that said, "My name is Goody Two Shoes," and, "I know a cat named Halloween." One after another, she pictured them in her mind until there was room for nothing else there, until she eventually fell asleep.

Seven

A Secret Collector

IN SPITE OF Amy's noble resolve that she and Michelle would be two against the world, when Hisa, Janie, and Barbara snubbed her in school, she was hurt. Then she pushed the whole business out of her mind to concentrate on a gift for Michelle's birthday. Something very, very special. Although she went shopping with her mother one afternoon, she found nothing suitable. Everything was either too expensive or not special enough. Finally her mother, worn out to the point of irritation, said, "I've had it! We must have covered thirty stores. You'll just have to find something in the neighborhood."

This gave Amy an idea. When they returned home, she headed right for the village. First, she tried The Sorcerer's Den. To her dismay, someone had already bought the earrings with the little glass balls. At the drugstore, she had no better luck. The golden hoops were gone, too. Amy told herself that it was all for the best. The idea was stupid anyhow. If Michelle was afraid to have her ears pierced, what would she do with the earrings? Amy would have to come up with something better.

That evening the answer presented itself. She and Michelle sat at Amy's desk in the bedroom doing homework together. Michelle, finally bored with early American heroes and their contributions to New World government, pushed her book aside, got up, and idly began to examine the open shelves of dolls. At first, Amy paid no attention, but when she saw Michelle pick up Aimee, lift her dress, and examine the doll's body, she demanded, "What are you doing?"

"I just wondered what it was made of."

"It's some kind of plastic."

Michelle tapped her finger against the material. "You're right." She pulled down the dress and carelessly returned the doll to the shelf. "You still want to get rid of it?"

For a moment, Amy was at a loss for words. Then she pretended to give her attention to her homework, mumbling an indistinct, "Mmmm."

"I said, 'Do you want to get rid of it?' "

Amy kept her eyes on her book as she said, "I don't see how I can. I don't know another doll collector."

"I do."

Surprised, Amy looked up. "You do?"

"Well, not exactly a doll collector. But I saw this store not too far from the village. It said 'Antiques and Dolls.'

Maybe we could walk over there some day. I bet you could get rid of it there. I bet you could even sell it to them."

"Sell it!" Amy said in a shocked voice. "I would never, never sell anything in my collection."

"You wouldn't?"

"Never!"

"Not even to me?"

"To you?" Amy stared at Michelle in disbelief. "That's the silliest question I ever heard. You don't want to buy a doll anyhow."

"Maybe I do."

Amy realized that she had said the wrong thing. Tell Michelle she didn't want something and, of course, she had to have it. Amy decided to call her bluff. "Okay. If you wanted to buy one of my dolls and if I wanted to sell one, which I don't, which one would you want?"

Michelle caressed her chin thoughtfully as her eyes scanned the shelves. "Well, I don't know—one that didn't cost too much, I guess." She began to walk up and down, now and then grabbing and examining a doll in the rough way that always made Amy so nervous. Amy got up and trailed her, hands ready, if worst came to worst, for a quick rescue. Each time Michelle shoved a doll back in place, or almost in place, Amy took a second to make the proper adjustments to clothes and positioning. She felt as anxious as a mother trying to keep one step ahead of her toddler in a china shop.

To Amy's great relief, Michelle finally stopped in front

of the display case and merely stared through the glass doors. "What are those?" She pointed to the little dolls carved out of wood.

"They're 'Penny Woodens.' " Amy went on to give their history.

"Wood, huh? I guess they wouldn't be too expensive." Michelle gave a quick nod. "Okay, I'll take one of those. How much?"

She sounded so serious, Amy was startled. "You really mean it?"

"Of course."

"But why would you want to buy one of my dolls? You don't even like dolls."

"Well," Michelle dragged out the word, apparently to cover a moment of thinking time. Then she said, "Well, if you want to know—I'd just like to have something to remember you by."

Now Amy was touched, really touched. Then a fearful thought struck her. "You're not going away, are you?"

"Well, no—not right now."

"When?"

"Well—well, sometime."

"When?"

"When? Well, how about when I go to college? Time passes pretty fast, you know. And I might go someplace far away—maybe even Europe. If I went to college in Europe, we might never see each other again. That's why I want something to remember you by."

Amy relaxed. That was a hundred years away. All the

same, she was touched. Michelle really did want something to remember her by. It made Amy feel a little choked up. Then she realized that she had just found the perfect gift for Michelle's birthday, a gift that would forever cement their friendship. But until Friday it would have to be kept secret. She tried to act as if she were solemnly considering the matter. "You know, I never thought I'd ever sell any of my dolls. And Penny Woodens are worth a lot more than a penny these days—a lot more." Michelle might as well know she wasn't getting some cheap gift. "I'd have to think about it."

"For how long?"

"Oh—a couple of days anyhow." Amy smiled to herself. Who knows? she thought. Michelle might even become a collector. Sometimes a gift of an old doll was all it took. "Now, I'm not promising anything, understand. I'm just saying I'll think about it."

"Maybe I could trade you something. Then you'd have something to remember me by, too."

"Trade me what?"

"Well, how about my Age of Aquarius poster?"

Now Amy was indignant. A dumb poster for a priceless collector's item? Then she remembered that Michelle was very fond of that poster. You might even say that, to her, it was a collector's item, too. Amy said again, "I'll have to think about it."

On the evening of Michelle's birthday, Amy left her carefully wrapped gift at home. She decided to give the doll to Michelle when they returned from Farrell's and could be alone. Now she made her way down the hall and knocked on the Mudds' door. When Michelle's mother answered, Amy said, "Michelle told me to come over when I was ready."

"Come in, Amy." Mrs. Mudd had on a long hostess gown. The silver hoops in her ears jounced around fascinatingly. "Michelle ran downstairs to see if her father was here. She'll be right back."

Michelle's father never came upstairs, Amy knew. Hugo and Michelle always met him in the lobby.

Amy followed Mrs. Mudd into the living room to find Double-Oh-Seven there. At least, that was what Michelle called him. When Amy had asked why, Michelle said, "Because all of my mother's boy friends are nothings. This one's a double nothing and he's her seventh." They'd had a good laugh about that.

From the sofa where he sat with a drink in his hands, Double-Oh-Seven eyed Amy indifferently. Mrs. Mudd's beautifully long-lashed eyes swept from Amy to him to a second drink on the coffee table and back to Amy. "Tell you what, Amy," she said. "Why don't you get Michelle's jacket from her closet and take it down to her. Then she'll be all set to leave when her father comes. Hugo's ready now. He's downstairs with her."

Amy didn't have to ask which jacket. Michelle, who usually cared nothing for clothes, was wildly excited about her mother's gift, a denim pants suit and matching hat, both decorated with silver nailheads. When she'd modeled the outfit for Amy, she'd said, "I can hardly wait for my birthday to wear it."

In the bedroom now, Amy decided that turning twelve must account for Michelle's new interest in clothes. And the interest had to be new. Michelle's messy closet was proof of that. There was more on the floor than on the racks. Amy rummaged through, yet she couldn't find the jacket. She was about to give up when she spotted its bottom showing beneath an old sweatshirt with "Frankenstein Died for Your Sins" written across the front.

Amy slipped everything off the hanger and slid the jacket out from under. When she replaced the sweatshirt in the closet, her eyes lit on the hat that matched the denim outfit, a big squashy cap with a peak and a pompon on top. It sat on the upper shelf wedged between an untidy jumble of boxes. Naturally Michelle would want the hat, too.

Standing on tiptoe, Amy could just reach the peak. She pulled, but the hat resisted her. Another tug and she realized why—but too late. The hat had been covering a cardboard box which now came crashing to the floor, spilling its contents all over. Amy stared down astonished.

The first thing that caught her eye was a big golden hoop. As she stooped to pick it up, she realized that the floor was covered with all kinds of earrings, all for pierced ears. There, too, was the pair with glass balls. Michelle had bought those and the hoops as well as so many others.

Why? She wouldn't even have her ears pierced. Then it flashed through Amy's head that Michelle, too, must be a collector. A secret collector? That seemed strange. Of course, if Michelle had admitted the truth to Amy, she'd have no reason to criticize Amy's doll collecting. And Michelle did like to criticize.

Although she felt smug in her knowledge, Amy had no time to sort out her thoughts. She quickly scooped up the earrings, deposited them in the box, and returned the box to the shelf. Then she took jacket and hat and made her way out. Let Michelle say just one more word about my dolls, she thought. Just one more word!

Eight

A Good Time Was Had by All

IT WAS DARK when Dr. Mudd, in the longest, whitest car Amy had ever seen, pulled up to the curb in front of the lobby. Amy, Michelle, and Hugo immediately ran out and piled into the back seat. As they started off, Michelle introduced Amy to her father and to his new girl friend, a Ms. Call-Me-Diana North. Amy had the impression of a big hulking man with a neatly clipped beard and, beside him, a much younger long-haired woman wearing a hat.

Michelle had waited until now to put on the things Amy had carried down to her. As she squirmed into the jacket, Hugo yelped, "Hey, watch it, Michelle! You nearly poked my eye out."

"Now, no squabbling, you kids," Dr. Mudd said indulgently. "Tonight we're all going to have a good time."

No one bothered to agree with him. Hugo began opening and examining ash trays. When he finished, he ran his fingers over the upholstery. "The new car is sure neat, Dad."

"Yeah," Michelle said as she mashed her hat on her head. "How much did it cost?"

Dr. Mudd said, "Michelle, you know better than to ask people what they've paid for something."

"Besides," Hugo said, "anybody knows how much Lincoln Continentals cost."

"How much?" she asked.

"Just about ten thousand dollars, that's all."

"Wow! That ought to keep you broke for a long time, Dad." Michelle certainly sounded hopeful.

Dr. Mudd took his eyes from the road just long enough to look over to the woman beside him and shake his head. "Kids!"

She gave a lovely throaty laugh which echoed through the car.

"She's a television actress," Michelle whispered to Amy. "They teach them how to laugh like that."

It took only minutes to reach Farrell's, a white and candy-cane red building ablaze with light. Hundreds of bare bulbs outlined the windows and even lit up the lot where Dr. Mudd parked. Michelle poked Amy with an elbow, said, "Watch this," then scrambled out of the car. Amy followed, wondering what Michelle was up to. In another moment, she had the answer. Call-Me-Diana stepped out and into the light. She wore a pants suit identical to Michelle's.

Grinning broadly, Michelle planted herself directly in front of her and said, "Surprise! How do you like it?"

The woman, seeming at a loss, stared at Michelle.

Then she turned to Dr. Mudd, who was now locking the car. "Is that why you told me to wear this outfit?"

He glanced around, a question in his eyes. It was a moment before he took in the situation. Then he began to laugh. Only Michelle joined him. Finally he said to her, "You sly puss. You should have told me what you had up your sleeve."

"You'd have told her. I wanted it to be a surprise." Michelle smiled at Diana. "The first time I met you you had it on. I told you I really loved it—remember?"

In a flat voice, Diana said, "I remember."

"Then I found one just like it in the mother and daughter department."

The woman's eyebrows shot up. "In I. Magnin's?"

"No. Sears, Roebuck."

Now Diana ran a cool appraising eye over Michelle's outfit.

"I wanted my mother to get one, too, but she said it wasn't her taste. She's very high fashion, you know. She said—"

Dr. Mudd quickly broke in with, "Mother and daughter department—didn't know they had such things." He gave Diana a meaningful look. "You know the old saw—imitation is the sincerest form of flattery."

"Oh, I'm flattered, all right. I'm really, really flattered," she said, not sounding flattered at all.

Amy heard him whisper, "Aw, come on—where's your sense of humor?"

"Given time, it may return."

Michelle graced Diana with her sweetest smile. "I just knew you'd be pleased."

At that point, Hugo, who had been examining the fine points of the car, joined them and they all started toward Farrell's, Amy and Michelle trailing the others.

Strange that the woman should have been offended, Amy thought. She herself would have adored it if she and Michelle had matching outfits. When she said so, Michelle stopped right in her tracks. Her palm slapped her forehead with such force she almost knocked the hat off her head. "Why didn't I think of that?" she moaned. "Oh, that would have been supergreat. She would have really flipped if we both had on pants suits like hers." Michelle began to giggle.

Amy realized for the first time that Michelle had deliberately set out to offend the woman. After a moment's thought, Amy decided, Why not? Who needed a stepmother anyhow? Amy was definitely on Michelle's side. She began to giggle with her.

Dr. Mudd glanced back suspiciously. He slowed the others until Michelle and Amy caught up. "Now, remember," he said in a tone that sounded threatening, "tonight we're all going to have a good time."

Inside Farrell's, there was a great to-do over where everyone should sit. Dr. Mudd wanted Michelle and Hugo at the ends of the table. Michelle would have none of it. To Amy's surprise, she insisted on sitting next to Diana. Amy wound up beside Hugo, leaving the head of the table to Dr. Mudd.

When he sat down, he glanced all around—at the red-flocked wallpaper, the Tiffany lamps, the bentwood chairs, the waiters in jaunty turn-of-the-century straw hats. He said to Diana, "What's all this supposed to be—some kind of early American decor?"

Diana smiled and Amy noticed that although the woman wasn't quite as young as she had first seemed, she was very pretty, with long red hair that gleamed in the light and eyes that crinkled at the corners. She said, "I'd say the decor was closer to early Disneyland."

With that, Michelle broke up with laughter. When it seemed as if she'd never stop, Hugo started laughing with her.

"That's enough," their father said.

Michelle took a moment to collect herself, then said, "I can't help it. She is *so* funny. Isn't she, Hugo?"

Diana, a half-puzzled, half-amused look on her face, said to Dr. Mudd, "I told you, given time, my sense of humor would return."

That sent Michelle into gales of laughter. Again Hugo joined her, the two looking as if they shared some private joke. Amy felt excluded.

Diana shrugged. "I always thought I was a dramatic actress, not a comedian."

Michelle and Hugo laughed all the harder.

Frowning now, their father said, "That's enough!"

Hugo promptly stopped. Michelle wiped the tears from her eyes, caught her breath, and said to Diana, "You're really witty, y'know?"

For the first time, Diana looked flattered. "Well, thank you."

The whole thing perplexed Amy. One minute Michelle seemed to hate the woman; the next minute, Michelle was falling all over her. Before Amy could give the situation any real thought, the waitress shoved a menu in front of her. Amy glanced up to find an exotic-looking young woman wearing a dazzling jewel in the middle of her forehead. Amy was enchanted. That almost seems better than pierced ears, she thought. She glanced over to Michelle to find her looking equally captivated.

When the waitress left, Michelle said, "Did you see that diamond?"

"Right in the middle of her forehead!" Amy said.

"That's really super."

Amy thought so, too.

"It's not a diamond," Diana said. "It's a rhinestone."

"It is?" Michelle still looked impressed. "I bet you'd have to have a hole cut in your forehead to keep something like that on."

"Glue," Diana said.

As she stared at Diana, Michelle's eyes filled with awe. "Really? I wouldn't have known that was a rhinestone—or about the glue. You know, you really are smart."

Diana's lovely television laugh was lost in the din of more urgent sounds from the far end of the room: first a drum roll, followed by a chorus of Happy Birthdays to a dear Michael, followed by the shrill of sirens, followed by the ringing of bells, followed by applause, followed by the wail of a baby.

"Oh, my God," Diana said. "I had no idea."

As lights flashed on and off, Michelle said, "Isn't it wonderful?"

"Fun," Amy said, although she wasn't quite sure she liked all that hubbub.

At that point, the waitress and her rhinestone returned to the table. Everyone but Michelle ordered cheese-burgers. After agonizing for several minutes over the choice between a "Tantalizing Turkey" or a Reuben sand-wich, she said, "I'll have both."

"Pig," Hugo said.

"She'll have turkey," her father said.

"Why can't I have both? It's my birthday. You're sup-posed to have what you want on your birthday."

"Michelle," her father said impatiently, "no one said you can't have what you want. But one at a time, please. I don't want to take you home sick."

"I won't get sick," she insisted. And after she finished her turkey, she proceeded to order a Reuben sandwich and to leave most of it uneaten.

"That's waste," Dr. Mudd said.

"My mother always used to remind me of all the starving children in Asia," Diana added.

Michelle said, "I'll tell the waitress to mail it to them."

"Don't be smart," her father warned.

"Well, it *is* my birthday. I should think a person

ought to be able to waste something on her birthday."

Hugo said, "It's my birthday, too. And *I'm* ready for dessert."

Dr. Mudd glanced at the menu again. "It seems they give you a free sundae on your birthday."

"You mean you're not going to buy us 'the Zoo'?"

"The Zoo?" Dr. Mudd ran his eyes down the menu until he located the item. "That serves ten people, Michelle. We could never eat that much ice cream."

She sank back into her chair with a sigh. "I knew it. It's just like Mom said."

Hugo squinted at her. "I didn't hear Mom say anything." He looked as if he knew what she was up to but still wanted to tease her.

"You weren't there at the time."

Dr. Mudd said, "What are you talking about? What did your mother say?"

Michelle glanced first at Diana, next at her father, then lowered her eyes. "I don't think I should say."

"Why?" Dr. Mudd asked.

"Well, I just don't think I should, that's all."

"Are you afraid it will embarrass me? Hurt my feelings?"

"It might."

"No, it won't. Go ahead and tell me what your mother said."

"I really don't think I should."

"No, go ahead—tell me. I want to know what's being said about me behind my back."

"Well—" Michelle paused, then said reluctantly, "Well, all right. I said you'd probably buy us the Zoo because it was our birthday. And she said—" She paused again. "You sure you want to hear this?"

"Go on, go on—tell me. What did she say?"

"She said you wouldn't buy us the Zoo because you're too cheap."

Dr. Mudd's beard and moustache covered a good portion of his face. What was left went as red as the flocking in the wallpaper. "Cheap!" He turned to Diana. "You hear that? Cheap! I just bought both of them color Sonys for their birthday. Now, I wouldn't exactly call that cheap, would you?"

She shook her head but said nothing.

Michelle said, "Oh, no. Those Sonys must have cost a lot of money—an awful lot. Maybe we'd better have the free sundaes."

"Cheap," Dr. Mudd muttered to himself, then fell silent until the waitress again appeared. Then he looked her straight in the rhinestone and, in an everyday voice, said, "One Zoo, please."

A short time later, with great fanfare, as the menu promised, two strong men came in bearing a stretcher of sorts and staggering under the weight of the enormous bowl full of all kinds of ice cream and sherbet. One of the men called to another passing waiter, "Give us a drum roll here."

The waiter sprang to the nearest drum. In the next instant, the sound reverberated through the room. This was

73

followed by a chorus of Happy Birthdays, followed by the scream of sirens, followed by the ringing of bells, followed by the flashing of hundreds of light bulbs.

Michelle grinned through the whole thing.

Although they did their best by the Zoo, when Amy saw the enormous amount left over, she felt a great pang of guilt over the starving children in Asia. A terrible waste, and all Michelle's fault. Yet no one could have looked more innocent and indifferent. Right now she was chattering to Diana about what a beautiful shade of red Diana's hair was. Amy saw Michelle stop suddenly and stare at the woman's shoulder.

Michelle said, "You have a loose hair on your jacket. Hold still. I'll take it off." She reached over and very deliberately yanked.

Diana jerked back with a yelp.

"Oh, I'm sorry," Michelle said. "I really thought it was loose."

Then Amy saw Michelle put the long hair in her napkin, fold the napkin, and place it in her pocket. Amy thought of hair and fingernail clippings and mind power.

All the while, voices on the public address system were singing, "Farrell's is fun for everyone. Farrell's is fabulous fun."

Nine

Never in a Million Years

MICHELLE'S DELIGHT OVER her birthday gift warmed Amy through and through. She felt the same saintly feeling you get when you've been wonderfully generous to someone less fortunate than yourself. Even if Michelle never became a doll collector, there was hope now that she would grow to understand others who had. That was why on the following day Amy suggested they investigate the antiques shop that Michelle had said carried dolls.

Michelle was willing. "Bring the doll your father sent you. Maybe you can get rid of it there."

"No," Amy said. "No, I don't think so. I'd have to haul it all that way and they might not have anything I wanted. I'll just see what they've got first."

The shop was a good distance from the village. As they walked, they talked about Michelle's father's girl friend. To Amy, Diana seemed nice enough. Michelle was of quite another mind. But Amy could understand that.

There were loads of "nice enough" women in the world, but who needed them for stepmothers? "What do you think you'll do about her?" Amy asked.

"I don't know. I just haven't decided yet."

The way Michelle avoided her eyes made Amy think that she had decided but wasn't about to tell anyone. Of course, it was magic Michelle was practicing. Perhaps it had to be kept secret—like wishing on a birthday cake or on a falling star. If you told someone, your wish would never come true.

The store looked a little like a junk shop with furniture jammed everyplace. Although a bell tinkled when they opened the door, no one seemed to be around. Amy spotted the dolls at the rear of the store. There were no moderns, she was pleased to notice. Although she never would admit it to Michelle, she had no intention of trading Aimee. Only two dolls interested her, a Gibson girl and a Kewpie. As she looked them over, she suddenly realized Michelle was not beside her. She was at the other end of the store, studying jewelry in a case.

Earrings? Amy wondered. She had given a great deal of thought to the box hidden in Michelle's closet and had decided, after all, that Michelle was not a secret collector. That made no sense. A more reasonable theory was that Michelle desperately wanted to have her ears pierced but her mother wouldn't allow it. She had already told Amy that much. So all Michelle could do was buy the earrings she wanted, look at them once in a while, and keep them ready for the day when her mother would have a change of heart. Poor Michelle.

In the next instant, Amy forgot all about poor Michelle and her earrings. On the counter near where Michelle stood, a glass case held one of the most interesting dolls Amy had ever seen. She quickly made her way over to it. "Why didn't you tell me?" she said to Michelle.

"Huh?" Michelle looked at Amy with a blank expression. "Tell you what?"

"Oh, that's a real museum piece," Amy said, her eyes glued to the doll in the case, a girl doll with long, curly blond hair wearing an old-fashioned children's dress. In one hand, she held a birdcage. Amy could see a little bird inside.

Suddenly a voice said, "You're quite right. She *is* a museum piece."

Amy glanced around to see a middle-aged woman coming through a rear door. In a brusque state-your-business-and-be-on-your-way tone, she said, "Something I can do for you girls?"

Michelle said, "Do you buy dolls?"

Amy said quickly, "They only have old dolls here."

"That's right. I buy old dolls. Do you have one to sell?"

"Oh, no. It's a modern," Amy said. "Practically a new doll."

"I'm afraid I wouldn't be interested. I deal in antique dolls."

77

"Well, that shoots that big idea," Michelle said. "Come on."

Amy hung back. She pointed to the doll with the birdcage. "Is that a French doll?"

The woman looked surprised. "How did you know?"

"The eyes mostly. Not that that proves anything. In those days, dollmakers in other countries *did* buy eyes from the French."

Michelle said to the woman, "She's a collector. She's got a bunch of old dolls. I bet you'd pay a lot of money to get some of them."

Now the woman was interested. Although Amy made it quite clear that she was selling nothing in her collection, the two had a marvelous conversation about dolls and dollmakers. Amy enjoyed herself thoroughly while Michelle stood by sighing with boredom. Amy didn't care. She ignored Michelle and began talking about the doll in the case. "She's so beautiful," Amy said.

"She's a mechanical doll," the woman told her.

"Really? Oh, I'd love to see her work. I don't have one mechanical doll in my whole collection."

After a pause the woman said, "Well, I don't usually do this—the doll is so old and fragile—but since you're a collector—" She opened the glass door, handled the doll for a moment, then stood aside. The little bird began hopping around in his cage, looking as if he were singing his heart out. When the mechanism finally ran down, Amy said, "Oh, that was wonderful. How much are you asking for the doll?"

"She's not for sale. She's part of my private collection. And you were right—she really belongs in a museum. She's very valuable."

When Amy and Michelle left the shop, Amy said, "I was kind of glad that doll wasn't for sale."

"Why?"

"Because I'd really love to have it. I might have been tempted to trade some of my dolls for it. I know I couldn't have come up with enough money to buy it—not something that valuable."

Michelle shrugged. "It can't be worth all that much. So the bird hops around. Big deal! It doesn't even sing. Besides, who needs it? Not you. You've got too many dolls already."

"Oh, you just don't understand," Amy said, starting to grow angry now. "And every time I talk about dolls, you don't have to act like I'm stupid or something."

"I don't act like you're stupid."

"Yes, you do."

"No, I don't. At least I don't mean it that way. I just mean that you've got practically every kind of doll there is now."

"I don't have a mechanical doll."

"Well, that's not exactly what I'd call a mechanical doll anyhow. It's only the bird that moves. And not all that much either."

Amy opened her mouth to answer, then thought better of it. What was the use? A little earlier she'd thought there was some hope for Michelle. She was wrong. Michelle would never understand. Never in a million years. And never in a million years would Amy mention dolls to her again!

When they came to the village, Michelle said she had some shopping to do. Amy begged off. Feeling more than a little cool toward Michelle now, she pretended that she had chores waiting for her at home. When they parted, Michelle never even seemed to notice how irked with her Amy was. Which irked Amy all the more. By the time she arrived home, she was in a really black mood.

Although it was Saturday, her mother was hard at work when Amy slammed the door. With the loud noise, the typewriter went quiet. "Is that you, Amy?" her mother called.

Amy sighed and aimed an impatient *yes* in the general direction of her mother's bedroom. To her surprise, she immediately heard the click of her mother's heels. In the next instant, her mother marched into the entry hall, a disturbed look on her face. "I want to talk to you, Amy," she said and motioned her into the living room. "Sit down."

She herself sat on the couch while Amy, expecting the worst, took her time settling into a chair across from her mother. Finally, in a wary voice, Amy said, "Talk about what?"

"About what you wrote to your father."

So that was it. He must have called while Amy was out. She scowled. "Well, I told you I didn't want to write to him. You said I had to."

"That wasn't quite what I said."

"Besides, I didn't ask him for that doll. I never asked him for anything. Just tell him not to send me things, and he won't hear what I have to say. And besides, I didn't want to write to him anyhow. And I wouldn't have if you hadn't made me."

Her mother gave a long sigh. "Amy, he *is* your father—and he loves you. All of which has nothing to do with how he feels about me or how I feel about him or anything else."

"Well, I don't want to talk about it."

Her mother was quiet for a moment. Then she said, "Well, like it or not, we're going to talk about it. And right now."

"I don't see why I have to talk about something I don't want to talk about. You never talk to me when I *do* want to talk about something."

"That's not true."

"It *is*. You're always too busy working. You care more about blending East and West for your old copy than about talking to me."

"Oh, for Pete's sake, Amy. That's simply not true."

"It is so. And if you want to know what I think, I think that's what caused the divorce." Amy saw her mother flinch slightly, yet she couldn't stop herself. The words she had bottled up inside for so long came tumbling out. "That, and because you're so sarcastic, and—and—" She could think of nothing more. Then it came to her, still another reason, and one she hadn't thought of before.

"And because you didn't have any more children."

Her mother's face flushed with anger now. "Amy, you don't know what you're talking about. You don't have the faintest notion—not the faintest—you just don't—" She broke off. Color drained from her face and a shadow passed over it. In a subdued voice she said, "Perhaps you do know what you're talking about in a strange kind of way. But it's not quite that simple."

Something in her mother's face, a hint of long hidden hurt, made Amy regret her outburst. But there was no taking it back now.

Her mother took a deep breath and let it out in a despairing sigh. "You're right, you know. All of the things you mention, and a good many more, contributed to the breakup. The thing is—and I don't want you to misunderstand—I'm not condemning your father. The fact is, I think we had too little in common. We simply didn't have the same values. He needed someone quite different, someone like his mother, a woman who dedicated herself to home and family. I simply couldn't do that. I've got too big an ego, I guess." She gave a little forced laugh. "You know, all along, I thought it was your father you blamed. It's really me, isn't it?"

Amy wasn't quite sure whom she blamed. In a sulky voice, she said, "At least you didn't leave. He did."

"Only because we both agreed that we weren't making it. We were two people who were compromising all that we held dear and hurting each other in the process."

"What about hurting me?"

"We considered you, Amy. Believe me, we did. But all three of us were involved. In the end, we decided that staying together would hurt us more than parting would hurt you."

"Nobody asked *me*," Amy said bitterly.

"Amy, it was a big hurt for me, too—my marriage a failure. But as time passes, I feel more strongly than ever that we were right to divorce. I *am* very work oriented, as you well know. And when I find my niche, whether it's right or wrong, I think that's going to mean as much to me as any marriage, perhaps even more."

"More than me, too, I bet."

"Oh, Amy—no. You're right about my not wanting more children. But I wanted you very much. I was an only child myself. Maybe that's why it seems natural to me to have only one. Besides, I've always felt that it's quality and not quantity that counts."

"Daddy wanted more, though."

Amy was only guessing, so it surprised her when her mother said, "Yes, he did."

And now he has them, Amy thought. A ready-made, instant family. The thought made her feel even more bitter toward him.

"You mustn't think that means he was in any way dissatisfied with you," her mother said. "He just happens to be the sort of man who likes kids and would enjoy having a flock of them."

"Well, he's sure got them now."

"You mustn't condemn him for being the way he is, nor me for being the opposite. We can't stop being the people we are."

"But I never even knew you were opposite. Nobody told me anything. Michelle says her mother and father fought all the time, yelled at each other, and everything. She wasn't even surprised when they got a divorce."

"Maybe it would have been better if we *had* yelled. And maybe we made mistakes in the way we handled things with you—I just don't know." Her mother stared anxiously into Amy's face. "That's all past. Now we both have to adapt to a new way of life."

"I never even knew there was anything wrong with the old one."

"It wasn't all bad, Amy. There were the good times, too. And there was you. I would have hated to have missed either. In spite of everything, I'd say it was like money well spent. At least, that's the way I think of it now."

Money well spent. What a strange way to remember a disaster.

Her mother said, "You can still have a relationship with your father, you know. He'd really like you to spend summer vacations with him."

Amy gasped. "And with *her?* And *her* kids?"

"Yes."

"Oh, no. Not me. Not ever."

"At least talk to him on the phone, Amy."

"No! Not ever, ever, ever."

Her mother stared at her with troubled eyes. At length she said, "You'll feel differently in time."

"Never," Amy said. Never in a million years.

Ten

Retribution

SEVERAL DAYS HAD passed since Amy and her mother had talked about the divorce. During that time, for some reason, Amy seemed to feel cross about everything. One evening she sat in her room, poring over a school book, growing more and more irritated. Michelle had promised to come to Amy's so that they could study together for a history test and she hadn't shown up. Then Amy remembered about Michelle's new color Sony. She was probably watching a good program. Amy decided to go to Michelle's apartment and watch with her. They could study later.

Amy told her mother where she was going, then took off for Michelle's. When she knocked on the Mudds' door, Hugo opened it. Without even greeting her, he pointed toward Michelle's bedroom and said, "She's watching TV."

As Amy set off down the hall, she could hear the Sony

blasting. I was right, she thought. But I'm not going to get mad about it. I'm absolutely not going to get mad about it. Anybody could get involved in a good show and forget she was supposed to be at somebody's apartment a half-hour ago. But she could at least call during a commercial.

Michelle's door was closed, which was unusual. Amy opened it, expecting to find her sprawled on the bed, her eyes fixed on the screen. To Amy's surprise, Michelle sat at her desk, deeply engrossed in hammering away at something. In another moment, Amy saw the something. And she couldn't believe it—wouldn't believe it.

She moved closer to the desk, feeling a little dazed. With lively music coming from the Sony, Michelle never even heard her. She finished hammering and held up her work, obviously to admire it.

Now Amy *had* to believe it. She could have cried. What had once been a dear little "Penny Wooden" in a peasant costume was now a grotesque image of what, Amy supposed, was meant to be Diana. Michelle had glued red yarn to the head for hair and, from her own denim pants suit, had made a crude outfit for the doll. Michelle's chopped-off pants lay on the floor beside her. Worst of all, the doll was scarred beyond repair, a huge nail driven clear through its middle.

"Oh, how could you?" Amy sputtered, her voice rising above the sound of the television. "How could you?"

Michelle whirled around in her chair, a stunned look on her face. Then her eyes darted to the clock on her desk, as if, until now, she'd forgotten all about time.

87

Amy felt the anger rising inside her. She opened her mouth to spit it out, then realized she couldn't talk above the television set. She ran and turned it off, then faced Michelle again. "How could you?"

With a guarded expression, Michelle glanced at the doll, then at Amy. "What do you mean?"

"You know what I mean. Why'd you have to ruin my doll?"

"What do you mean—*your* doll? You gave it to me."

"And I wouldn't have if I'd known what you wanted it for. You said you wanted something to remember me by. Oh, what a liar you are, Michelle."

"Who's a liar? I did want something to remember you by."

"Then why did you ruin it?"

"Who ruined it? I just made some different clothes for it."

Amy looked again at the doll and felt sick. "Ruined," she murmured. "You had no right."

"You gave me the doll. If you give something to somebody, she ought to be able to do what she wants with it."

"And that was my favorite. I just didn't give you any old Penny Wooden, Michelle. I gave you my favorite, my very favorite."

Michelle lowered her eyes. "You didn't tell me it was your favorite. But what difference does that make? Why shouldn't I do what I want with it?"

"Because that's an antique doll. And it's valuable. At least, it was until you spoiled it."

Michelle said, sullenly, "Well, if you hadn't barged

in on me like that you wouldn't have even known."

"Oh, Michelle—that just shows how much you think of our friendship."

"What do you mean? I think as much of our friendship as you do."

"Oh, no, you don't. I really valued our friendship. I really did. But you betrayed me."

"Aw, come on—"

"I mean it. You lied to me. Oh, I feel sorry for you, Michelle—you just don't seem to know what's important and what's valuable. You knew if you hurt that doll, it would be just like hurting me. But did that stop you? No."

"I wasn't trying to hurt *you*. I was trying to hurt somebody else."

"I didn't mean it that way. And I know what you're trying to do and who you're trying to do it to—Diana. And I have to tell you—I think that's evil!"

Michelle, a scowl on her face, opened her mouth, obviously to defend herself, but Amy went right on, "You and me—we just don't have the same values. In fact, I really don't think we have anything in common at all. And what's more, I'll never forgive you for what you did. And what's more, I don't want to talk to you ever again!"

Before Michelle could respond, Amy fled from the room and out the apartment door, her eyes a blur. She tore down the hall, not seeing much of anything in front of her. Near the elevator, she stumbled over something. She heard a pained cry and looked down to find Mousy Tongue, back arched, giving her a hostile stare.

89

Amy cried, "Oh, you poor Mousy. You poor, poor Mousy." She knelt down, murmuring apologies, stroking his back until he finally relaxed. Then she picked him up and hugged him.

Poor, poor Mousy. She had hurt him. "Oh, I'm so sorry—so sorry," she said as the tears rolled down her cheeks. "I didn't mean it. Honest, I didn't."

To make it all up to Mousy, she pushed the button to summon the elevator. When the door finally opened, she set him inside the car. He turned around to face her, his blue eyes staring up at her as if to say, Nothing's worth making that much fuss about.

Amy reached inside the elevator and pressed the lobby button. As the door closed, she said, "Oh, Mousy, you don't know how lucky you are to be a cat."

Eleven

A Real-Life Corny Game Show

AMY WHEELED THE portable television set into her bedroom. Four days had passed since she had spoken to Michelle. She turned on a rerun of "Gilligan's Island," taking some satisfaction from the realization that she could watch it without hearing comments from Michelle. It was a corny program, Michelle always said. If she were watching, she would have insisted on a game show. They were corny, too, Michelle admitted, but that was all right because they were real-life corn. There was a difference between real-life corn and made-up corn.

Amy never quite understood the distinction. When she had tried to get Michelle to explain, Michelle had said, "That's the kind of thing that if you have to have it explained, you wouldn't understand anyhow."

Damn Michelle. It was better to have no friends than one like her.

And it looked as if that was exactly what Amy was

going to wind up with—no friends. It was late in the school year to make new friends now. Because of Michelle, she had cut herself off from the others, even made enemies of some. And the sad part was that they all seemed to live very comfortably without her.

At one point, Amy had thought of confiding in her mother. While she was thinking about it, the agency had given her mother a new account, and now mom was so busy she hadn't even noticed Michelle's absence around the apartment. It was just as well, Amy thought. Mom would only ask why Amy hadn't tried harder to make friends with Barbara and some of the others.

More than once in school Amy had thought Michelle was about to speak to her. Each time, she made a point of avoiding Michelle's eyes or of deliberately moving away from her. Even if I *am* lonely, Amy decided, there are more important things than loneliness. Principles, for instance.

Amy was deep into "Gilligan's Island" when she heard the front door knocker. Mrs. Lovelace, Mousy Tongue's owner, had borrowed eggs in the afternoon. She was probably returning them now.

Amy listened for a moment to see if her mother would answer. The typewriter continued clicking away, so Amy got up to go to the door herself. When she opened it, instead of Mrs. Lovelace, there stood Michelle, arms behind her back, a meek look on her face.

"Hi," Michelle said.

In spite of herself, Amy was pleased. Yet she kept her voice cool. "Hi."

"I didn't use our special knock."

Amy lifted her eyebrows in an expression that suggested she had never heard of their special knock. Or had forgotten.

"Yeah. I figured if you knew it was me, you wouldn't let me in."

What could Amy say to that? Nothing. The two stood there staring at each other in a long, uneasy silence. At length, Michelle said, "Can I come in? I've got something for you."

For some reason, whatever Michelle had she was holding behind her. "If it's the ball-point pen I left in your apartment, you didn't have to bother."

"Ball-point pen? Oh, no, it's not that. Maybe I'd better come in." When Amy failed to move aside, Michelle said, "Well, can I?"

"Come in?"

"Yes."

Amy shrugged. "It really doesn't make any difference to *me*."

"Then I'll come in." Michelle, keeping her arms behind her, edged by Amy. "Let's go to your room."

Amy shrugged again. "If you want to."

Michelle followed Amy down the hall. In the bedroom, she glanced toward the television set and almost accusingly said, "You were watching 'Gilligan's Island.' "

Amy had forgotten all about "Gilligan's Island." She hastily turned the set off. "I wasn't watching anything. I'd just turned it on when you knocked on the door." How could you admit to someone you were watching something which that very same someone called corny?

There was another long moment of silence. Finally Michelle drew her hands from behind her. "This is what I wanted to give you." She held out the "Penny Wooden" which, only a few days before, Amy had thought was ruined. Now it looked as if Michelle had never touched it. The yarn had disappeared from its head and it was dressed again in its peasant costume.

Michelle lifted the dress. "I filled the hole with some plastic wood that Hugo had. Then I sanded it. You can hardly tell." The expression in her eyes asked Amy to agree with her. When Amy said nothing, she added, "The yarn was stuck on with water-base glue. It came right off when I wet it. Looks just like it did before." Again she looked at Amy with the same expression. Amy said nothing. Finally Michelle held the doll out to her and said, "Here."

Amy, perplexed now, made no move to take it. "I don't understand—"

"I'm giving it back to you."

"Giving it back? How come?"

"Well, I just got to thinking it was a real shame to break up your collection."

It was unlike Michelle to worry about Amy's collection. Amy said, "The doll was your birthday present. I couldn't take it back now."

"But I really want you to have it."

"That just wouldn't be right. You can't give somebody something for her birthday, then take it back. Besides, I don't think you care anything about my collection anyhow."

"You don't?"

"No, I don't. So I don't understand why you're giving it back."

Michelle took a moment to think about it. Then she said, "The thing is, the doll means a lot more to you than it does to me. I think you should have it. Besides, it's valuable. It wouldn't be right for me to accept a gift that valuable."

Amy peered at Michelle, looking for some indication of sarcasm. No, Michelle looked perfectly serious. "I'm glad you realize the doll is valuable, but I still can't take back something I gave you for a birthday present."

For once, Michelle looked at a loss. "Oh," she said.

A real impasse. They both fell silent and stared at the Penny Wooden which had now become a symbol of their broken friendship. Broken? Or, like the doll, only scarred?

Amy suddenly had a brilliant thought. "Maybe I could buy you something else for your birthday—I mean, instead of the doll."

Michelle's face brightened. "Oh, that's a good idea," she said eagerly. "A really good idea."

"But what?" Amy asked.

"What? Well, I don't—well, I guess there's a lot—well, how about a poster? I could really use a new poster for my room. In fact, I'd really love something like that."

Amy hesitated. "Well, if you really think you'd want one. I mean, if you're not just thinking up just anything to make it easy for me."

"Oh, no—I wouldn't do that. I really want a poster. I mean, there's this poster I've been wanting for a long time." She thrust the doll toward Amy.

Amy only stared at it. "Honest? You really want a poster?"

"I swear I do."

"Well—well, okay." Amy took the doll from Michelle's hands. "But I'd better get the poster tomorrow. I wouldn't feel right if I didn't get it right away."

"Okay."

Amy played with the doll's dress as she said, "If you'll tell me which poster you want, I'll go look for it after school." She paused. "Of course, sometimes it's kind of hard to tell one of those posters from another."

"It really is," Michelle agreed.

"I sure hope I don't get the wrong one."

As Amy knew she would, Michelle said, "I could go with you."

"Oh, that's a good idea. Then I won't make any mistakes."

Another silence. Michelle stood there, shifting from

one foot to the other. After a moment, she said, "I'm sorry I interrupted your television show."

"That's okay. I wasn't watching anything special."

"There's a good show on now," Michelle offered.

"What channel?"

Michelle scratched her head. "You know, I just can't seem to remember. I bet I could find it for you though."

"Oh, okay."

While Michelle fiddled with the set, Amy placed the Penny Wooden back in the case with the other old dolls. She had been so relieved to find the doll restored almost to its former state that she'd nearly forgotten the purpose Michelle had intended for it. "Whatever happened with the whammy you were putting on Diana?" she asked now.

"Oh, that. Well, I found a better way to do it."

Concerned, Amy said, "I hope it's not like with the doll. I mean, I hope you're not trying to do something bad to her—I mean, like kill her."

"Kill her! I wasn't trying to kill her. I was just trying to make her a little sick, because my dad hates to be around sick people."

Amy felt slightly relieved. "What are you doing now?"

"Well, I made this pentagram—that's a five-pointed star. It's a lot more powerful than a doll. You put all these secret symbols on it and the person it's meant for has to do what you want her to."

"Like what?" Amy asked, still suspicious.

"Nothing bad," Michelle assured her. "I just put some

symbols on it to make her feet wander. That way, she'll wander right out of my father's life, I figure."

That didn't sound bad at all. As Amy watched Michelle tune the set, she wondered what would have happened to the little Penny Wooden if Michelle had not come up with a more powerful magic. Would she have given it back anyhow?

But why borrow trouble? From the outside, the doll looked as good as ever. And Diana was safe from violence. Everything was very much the way everything had always been. Or, like the doll, almost. And Amy was so so glad.

Without another word about their rift, Michelle sat on the bed, the portable television set pulled around to face her. "Come here," she said to Amy and patted the bedspread beside her. "You've just got to see this show—it's new."

Amy joined Michelle and they both settled back to watch a real-life corny game show.

Twelve

With a Little Help from Jackie Kennedy

FOR A WHILE Amy and Michelle drifted back into the same old relationship—sometimes comfortable, sometimes uncomfortable. Then one Sunday when Michelle and Hugo visited their father, Michelle didn't look in on Amy as she normally did afterward. Amy supposed that she had gotten home too late.

Monday morning at the usual time Amy knocked on the Mudds' door. Michelle opened it and peered out.

"Ready for school?" Amy asked.

"Not quite." Michelle hesitated for the briefest second, then said, "Why don't you go on ahead? I'll only make you late."

Amy wondered what had gotten into Michelle. Certainly she never cared if she made someone else late. "That's okay—I'll wait for you."

Michelle frowned and chewed on her lip the way she always did when she was considering the best way to attack a problem. Amy was beginning to get the feeling that she just might be the problem.

Finally Michelle said, "I'm not going to be able to walk to school with you today. I've got to wait for Hugo."

Strange. Michelle and Hugo never walked to school together. "It's still early. I'll wait with you," Amy offered.

Michelle said quickly, "Oh, no, you don't have to do that."

"I don't mind."

Michelle shifted uneasily. "Well, to tell you the truth, we've got things we've got to talk about alone—Hugo and me."

"Oh," Amy said, taken aback.

Michelle's uncomfortable look left her now. Instead, she seemed to puff up with importance. "Yeah, we got real personal things to talk about—private, y'know?" She might as well have given Amy a pat on the head as she added, "You understand."

Run along, little girl. The big kids don't have time for you. Was that what Michelle was trying to tell her? Amy was so stunned that she didn't know how to react. All she could think of to say was, "I'll see you in school then."

It wasn't until she was halfway there that she realized how hurt she was. Until now, Amy had believed she and Michelle had no secrets from each other. What had changed?

By lunchtime, Amy had not entirely recovered from her hurt. Still, she was trying to look at things sensibly. It was probably all a big joke. Undoubtedly a joke. She'll tell me everything while we're having lunch, Amy thought. We'll have a good laugh about it.

Amy was wrong. Michelle had no intention of telling her anything at lunch. "Hugo and I are eating together," Michelle said. "You don't mind, do you?"

Amy knew she was again being excluded. And, again, she was so surprised that all she could do was shake her head.

After school it was the same thing. Michelle was going to walk home with Hugo, and Amy was not invited—not even given an explanation. And as if that wasn't enough of a slap in the face, Michelle said, "Oh, yeah—and don't wait for me tomorrow morning. I'll be going to school with my brother."

And every morning after that, Amy guessed. Well, nobody had to drop a ton of bricks on *her* head before she got the message. She was hurt, but she was also angry.

Instead of heading for home and taking a chance on running into Michelle and Hugo, Amy killed time in the school library. She wandered through shelves of books, not seeing any of them for the mist in her eyes. All she could think about was Michelle's sudden and bewildering change.

Amy searched her memory for something she had done to make Michelle angry. She could think of nothing. Then it must be something about me, she decided. Her mind reviewed every offensive human condition that television had ever warned against. But if she'd had bad breath or body odor or anything like that, her mother would have been the first one to tell her. No, it must be something else.

At one time Hugo and Michelle had been very close, Amy knew. Practically inseparable, Michelle had said. She had also said, and with a touch of pride in her voice, that they hadn't even needed anyone else. Of course, they were twins and twins often had a special closeness. Yet, to Amy, they had never seemed like twins, but more like any other brother and sister.

For some reason, Hugo was again willing to have Michelle for a companion. And now that she had Hugo, Michelle needed no one else. Not even Amy. That must be the reason. *Had* to be the reason. Maybe it had something to do with turning twelve. And I really valued our friendship, Amy thought. I really did. Now she felt not only sorry for herself but wronged.

She might have gone right on nursing her grievance had she not spotted Barbara, Hisa, and Janie, who were all about to check out books. Something about the sight of them giggling together made Amy feel more lonely than ever.

There was a long-ago time when she would have been one of those giggling girls. Now she was an outcast. What had happened to her? The divorce, for one thing. But something else as well. Michelle. Michelle had happened to her. Or worse. She had let Michelle happen to her.

Amy, without the slightest idea of what she meant to do about it, picked up a book. Without even looking at the title, she made for the checkout desk to take a place in line behind Barbara. She stood there wondering, What now? Then she noticed the title of Barbara's book. *Sounder.* Although Amy had never read the book, she had seen the movie. She wasn't quite sure whether she was swallowing her pride or a hard lump as she said, "That's a good book."

Barbara, with her usual sweet smile, glanced around. When she saw Amy, the smile faded.

Instead of letting Barbara's attitude daunt her, Amy plunged right in. She nodded toward the book. "That's a really good book, *Sounder.*"

Automatically, Barbara said, "It is?" Then she glanced quickly toward Hisa and Janie as if expecting them to chide her for speaking to Amy. They were too busy juggling books to notice.

"Oh, yes—really good. But it's sad," Amy said.

"It is?"

"Oh, yes. I cried." It was the movie that had made Amy cry, not the book. But that was neither here nor there. The story had to be the same. "I just cried and cried."

"You did?"

"Oh, yes." Before Amy could venture anything further, the line moved. As Barbara turned away to shove her book toward the librarian, she looked almost relieved.

Amy bit her lip. The overture had taken everything she had, yet nothing had come of it. When it was her turn at the desk, she watched Barbara join the other girls. She knew she could catch up with them if she wanted to. But what if they ignored her? Or said something as mean to her as she had said to them? Oh, she would be so embarrassed. And, of course, there were three of them to egg each other on. They could really crucify her if they wanted to.

But hadn't she been feeling crucified all day? Or something just as bad. How could she feel any worse? When the librarian passed back her book, Amy grabbed it, tore out of the building and after the three girls.

"Hey, you guys," she said as she caught up and fell into step beside them. Trying to act as if they were all old pals, she asked, "You still want to see my doll collection?"

For a moment they stared at her in surprise.

Amy said anxiously, "How about it?"

No one spoke. Then Barbara glanced at Janie with an expression that begged her to take over. When it was obvious Janie was not up to that responsibility, both girls' eyes lit upon Hisa. Amy followed the glances, feeling as if she were watching a game of Pass the Buck.

With three pairs of eyes turned on her now, what could Hisa Nakata do but try to rise to the occasion? She tossed her long, gleaming hair with just the right amount of haughtiness and said, "What doll collection is that? I never heard of any doll collection, did you, Janie?"

Ah. Hisa, looking mighty pleased with herself, had

pointed the way. Now Janie had no trouble following. "No, I never heard about any doll collection. Did you, Barbara?"

Barbara, less quick on the uptake, said, "You remember, I told you all about it the day after—" She caught herself, obviously aware from the cool glances of the others that she had goofed.

Amy said quickly, "Well, I don't suppose there's any reason to remember about my collection. After all, it's only a bunch of dolls—kachinas and corncobs and 'Penny Woodens.' And, of course, my French Fashion doll and my peddler. I mean, it's only a lot of antique dolls with china or papier-mâché or bisque heads. And my modern dolls—anybody could have seen those anyhow."

When Hisa and Janie exchanged glances, Amy hoped that she was whetting their interest. "I don't suppose you'd want to see it, but if you did, you could all come over this afternoon." The moment she said the words, she wondered if the living room was picked up, if there was something to eat in the house, something to drink. Well, she would just have to risk it. "I'd really love to have you."

They all looked a little wary. After a moment's hesitation, Hisa said, "Well, I really don't think I want to see a doll collection. Do you, Janie? I mean, she's right. We've all seen kachinas and old dolls before."

"Oh, sure. I've seen lots of kachinas," Janie said.

"Did you ever see a French Fashion doll or a peddler?" Amy asked.

Hisa shrugged. "Oh, well—"

Janie shrugged. "Oh, well—"

Although Amy suspected they had certainly never seen the like of her dolls, she had no argument for them. If a French Fashion and a peddler couldn't make them change their minds, what could? Nothing.

She felt completely depressed now. At the moment not even her dolls seemed of any value. In a gloomy voice, she said, "I guess there isn't any reason why anyone should want to see them. After all, they're only dolls. I don't even have any limited editions except Jackie Kennedy."

"Jackie Kennedy?" Hisa said.

"Jackie Kennedy?" Janie said.

"I forgot about Jackie Kennedy," Hisa said.

"Me, too," Janie said.

Maybe all was not lost. Quickly, Amy said, "You might never get a chance to see another Jackie Kennedy. They only made five hundred."

Barbara said, "Oh, you'd just love her Jackie Kennedy. She's so so beautiful."

Hisa and Janie again exchanged glances, long meaningful glances.

Then Barbara said, "Oh." The word had a flat, ugly sound as if she had just remembered something distasteful. "What about Michelle?"

"Michelle?" Amy acted as if she had never heard of Michelle.

"Will she be there?"

"Michelle? Oh, no. I have no idea where Michelle

is—or will be." And I couldn't care less, Amy's attitude suggested.

That seemed to satisfy Barbara. She said to Hisa and Janie, "I wouldn't mind seeing her collection again if you two want to."

Hisa said to Janie, "You want to?"

Janie said, "I don't know. Do you want to?"

"I asked you first."

Janie had to think about that. But she finally came up with the all-time perfect answer. "I want to if you want to."

Amy contained a sigh of relief. She had battled it through and won. But not without a little help from Jackie Kennedy.

Thirteen
Whatever Happens, It's All Your Fault

AMY HAD ALMOST forgotten how much fun it was to be with a group of girls. She was especially delighted to learn that she was not the only collector in the bunch. Barbara collected figures of owls, and Hisa collected autographed pictures of rock stars. Even Janie had begun a shell collection. Unlike Michelle, not one of the three seemed to think there was anything strange about collecting dolls. Amy thoroughly enjoyed the afternoon.

Before the girls left the apartment, Hisa said, "I still have all my old dolls. If you want to, after school tomorrow, you can come over and see them."

"Oh, I'd love to," Amy said, grateful that they all seemed so ready to forget her earlier rudeness.

On the following day, Michelle was again tied up with Hugo, but Amy never really missed her. Instead, she was more aware of a strange feeling inside herself. Somehow it made her think of when she was recovering from flu. For a while, staying at home was fun. When everyone was hard at work in school, she was reading books, watching television, and eating all the delicacies that were supposed to tempt an indifferent appetite. Then as the days dragged on, her room began to seem unbearable. She grew sick of looking at the pink and orange flowered wallpaper and at the fine crack running along one end of the plaster ceiling, sick of counting the dainty holes in the eyelet bedspread. Only conversation with her dolls had helped her bear up.

Then, at long last, came that glorious day when she could again step outdoors. Oh, how blue the sky was, how fresh the air. And all the world so lost behind the walls of her room—oh, how beautiful. She didn't want to think about why she had the same feeling today and why, oddly enough, it made her feel guilty.

That afternoon she walked home with Hisa who, it turned out, lived in a house on the next street over. Amy met Hisa's mother, a brother who was a high school junior, and all of Hisa's childhood dolls. Some of them were worth more now than when they were new, Amy told her.

"Even my Barbie doll?" Hisa asked.

"Oh, yes. And she'll be worth more every year." Amy had an idea it wouldn't take much for Hisa to turn into a doll collector. She had saved every one of her dolls and most were in good condition. What fun it would be to have one friend who was interested in the same thing you were interested in.

Hisa kept her dolls safely tucked away in boxes. Amy

said, "One thing I wish I had for my dolls is a dollhouse—one big enough to fit them."

"You could make one," Hisa suggested.

"Make one? I never really thought of that."

"You could use cardboard boxes for rooms and paint them and wallpaper them."

Hisa was full of advice. Even better, off her garage there was a big added room where she said Amy could work. "We call it the project room," Hisa told her. "My mother does all kinds of things with tiles and my brother pots."

"Pots?"

"I mean he makes pots out of clay. Anyhow we can work out there. We won't have to worry about making a mess."

"We?" Amy said.

"Sure. I'll make a dollhouse, too, for my dolls. Barbara and Janie can help if they want to."

"Oh, that will really be fun."

Hisa seemed as enthusiastic about the idea as Amy. That same evening after dinner they had several long phone conversations and made elaborate plans for the whole project, Hisa donating her brother's services to help with furniture. Amy couldn't remember a time when she'd felt more excited about anything.

The next morning she circled around the block to meet Hisa, and they walked to school together, still making plans. There were all sorts of things to figure out.

What would they use for rugs? For fireplaces? For lamps? For a hundred other things?

After school, along with Barbara and Janie, they headed for the village, where Janie's uncle owned a paint store. He contributed two wallpaper books of discontinued patterns to the project. Amy helped carry them to Hisa's house.

Amy knew her mother was working at home that afternoon, so she called to ask permission to stay at Hisa's for a while. To her surprise, someone else answered the phone. At first, Amy thought she had dialed wrong. In another moment, the voice registered. "Michelle?"

"Amy Warner! Where are you?"

What was Michelle doing in her apartment? "Where's my mother?" Amy asked.

"She'll be right back. She went to the store," Michelle said. "I've been waiting for you. Where are you?"

"I'm—why were you waiting for me?"

"I wanted to see you. What else?"

"Why'd you want to see me?"

"I'll tell you when you get here."

"You'd better tell me now because I'm not coming home for a while."

"Oh," Michelle said, sounding let down. After a moment, she added, "Well, I was just going to tell you to stop by my apartment in the morning. We can walk to school together."

Tell me to stop by? Amy thought. Order me to stop

by is more like it. "What's the matter with Hugo?"

"What do you mean, what's the matter with Hugo?"

"I mean, aren't you walking to school with him?"

"Uh uh," Michelle grunted. "He's meeting that kid he usually goes in with."

I might have known, Amy thought. For some reason she doesn't have Hugo anymore, so now I'm good enough. It gave Amy some satisfaction to say, "I'm sorry, but I won't be able to walk to school with you tomorrow."

For a moment, Amy thought that the line had gone dead. Finally Michelle said, "How come?"

Now it was Amy's turn to treat Michelle exactly as Michelle had treated her. "Because I'm going in with somebody else."

There was a long silence. Then Michelle said, "Who?"

Amy hesitated. Then she realized that there was no way to make a secret of it anyhow, so she said, "Hisa."

"Her! I thought you weren't even speaking to her."

"Well, I am."

There was another long silence. Finally Michelle said, "I can understand how somebody might get herself into something like that. I mean, I can see how if some-body made an appointment with somebody—even if she didn't like the somebody—she'd have to keep it. That's only right. You go ahead and do whatever you said you'd do. We'll walk home together after school."

Now she's giving me permission, Amy thought indignantly. "I won't be going home after school."

"Why not?"

"Because."

"Because why?" Michelle demanded.

"Look, Michelle—Hisa and I have an important project going. We'll be working on it every afternoon for a while."

"Project? What kind of project?"

"Oh—it's just not the kind of thing that would interest you."

"How do you know it wouldn't?"

"I just know. And Hisa and I'll have a lot of plans to make on the way to school—on the way home, too. We'll probably be talking about it all the time. You'd just be bored."

"Oh, I get it. What you mean is, Bug off!"

"I didn't say anything like that, Michelle."

"Now, wait a minute. Let me get this straight. What you mean is you don't want me for a friend anymore."

Now Amy started to feel guilty about what she was doing. "I didn't mean that."

"Okay, if you didn't mean that, just answer me one question. And you better think about it real hard before you say anything, because our whole future friendship depends on what you say."

Feeling uneasy, Amy said, "What's the question?"

"The question is, Are you going to school with me tomorrow?"

"I told you I wasn't."

"I know what you told me. I'm giving you a chance to

change your mind. I'll give you until I count to ten."
Michelle slowly began to count. If Amy had had a mo-
mentary pang of regret, by the time Michelle reached five,
it had dissolved into anger. Michelle finished counting
and said, "Okay, you wanna change your mind?"

"Michelle, I told you—"

"Yes or no?"

"*No!*"

A deadly silence fell. Then in a menacing tone, Michelle said, "Whatever happens, Amy Warner, it's all your
fault. You just remember that."

"What do you mean?"

Instead of an answer, Amy heard a harsh click. She
stood there for a moment, feeling chilled. Then she shook
off the feeling and rejoined Hisa. After all, Michelle's
threat was only a way of getting rid of anger, Amy assured
herself. Besides, it wasn't really a threat. "Whatever happens . . . it's all your fault" could mean anything. It
needn't mean Michelle meant Amy any harm. It could
even mean, When they find me dead, just remember that
you drove me to it.

Amy found that thought equally disturbing. Her afternoon was ruined now. She told Hisa that she was feeling a
bit sick, which was the truth, then hurried home. For the
rest of the day and the evening she worried about what
Michelle had in mind. It wasn't until bedtime that she
found out.

Amy was getting into her pajamas when she noticed

that Aimee was missing from her usual place on the shelf. Amy searched the other shelves, wondering why she couldn't remember moving the doll. Finally, she was about to go out and ask her mother if she knew what had happened to it when she noticed the curious lump in the bed.

A sudden fear seized Amy. She had all she could do to force herself to turn back the spread. There against the pillow was what was left of Aimee. The big nail driven through her dress had shattered her plastic middle.

"When they find me dead"? If Michelle ever considered killing anyone, it would never be herself. A great wave of nausea swept over Amy. In the next moment, she was sick.

Fourteen
What Are Friends For?

"IT MUST HAVE been the pork we had for dinner. It was much too fatty," her mother said and made Amy stay in bed all the next day.

Amy hadn't bothered to disagree. She was too weak. Then, too, there was something petrifying about finding out that someone wished you dead. Even more petrifying was the knowledge that the person wanted you to know she wished you dead. You had to think hard about something like that before you could even decide how to tell someone.

Amy had no doubt about Michelle's message and its meaning. After all, Michelle had been with her when the doll arrived. They had talked about Amy's father's note and about the doll's resemblance to Amy. Then, of course, there was the doll's name, so close to her own.

Later, when she felt better, Amy decided she would talk things over with her mother. Now all she wanted to do was to stay in bed and try to make her mind a blank. Which wasn't easy. She kept telling herself her upset stomach was only a coincidence, but the whole thing depressed her—not because she really believed a nail driven through a doll could kill her, but because she realized Michelle wished it could. Knowing something like that could make anyone die a little.

A good part of the day she slept. By midafternoon, her stomach began to feel better. Yet every time she thought of the ruined doll, she was heartsick. Because she couldn't bear to look at Aimee, she had laid the poor doll out of sight in a dresser drawer. Her casket, Amy thought now, and she felt an overwhelming sadness.

She was so deeply wrapped in despair she was unaware that anyone had knocked at the front door until she heard her mother talking to someone in the hall. "She's not contagious—just a stomach upset," her mother said. "Go in but don't stay too long."

The next thing she knew the last person whom Amy expected to see came hurrying into her room. Feeling dazed, Amy watched Michelle make for the bed, then stop short and stare speechlessly at her. If Amy looked wan, Michelle looked ghastly as she stood there biting her lower lip. In another moment, the corners of her mouth sagged. Tears flooded her eyes, spilled over, and rolled down her cheeks. "Oh, you really *are* sick," she said.

Amy had never seen Michelle cry before. The sight made unexpected tears well up in her own eyes.

"Oh, Amy—I'm sorry." Michelle's voice was a thin, pitiful wail. "I'm so so sorry. I didn't mean it. Honest, I didn't. Oh, I'll never forgive myself—never."

Amy opened her mouth but no sound came out.

Tears continued to stream down Michelle's cheeks. "When I saw you weren't in school, I knew what had happened. And it's all my fault—I made you sick. Oh, I'll never forgive myself."

Amy finally found her voice. "I'm all right."

Michelle paid no attention. "But it's not too late. I'll take it out now and the spell will be broken."

Amy didn't have to ask what Michelle meant to take out. "I already took it out."

"You did?" For a moment, Michelle almost looked thwarted. Then she said, "Oh, thank God!" She walked closer and stared down at Amy, her eyes red behind her aviator frames. "You'll never forgive me, will you?"

Amy said, "It was a terrible, terrible thing to do."

Michelle bit her lip again. "I know it was. But you really hurt my feelings. You really did."

"What about my feelings? You didn't care before when you hurt my feelings."

Michelle, looking completely innocent, lifted her glasses, wiped her eyes, sniffled, and said, "When was that?"

"You know when. I was only doing the same thing to you that you did to me with Hugo. When you had him, I wasn't good enough for you."

Michelle's face took on an injured expression. "How could you think a thing like that?"

"Because it's true."

"Oh, you are *so* wrong. You just can't imagine how wrong you are."

"I am?"

"Oh, yes. What you don't know is we had an important problem to talk about—Hugo and me."

"What problem?"

"A family problem. How could I burden you with a family problem?"

Michelle had never kept problems, family or otherwise, to herself before. Amy said, "I don't believe you."

Now Michelle really looked injured. "But it's true." Then her eyes dropped and she gave a sad sigh. "I wish it wasn't."

Amy began to get the feeling that Michelle just might be sincere. "What's true?"

Michelle said dully, "My dad and Diana—they're going to get married."

For the first time that afternoon, Amy felt a touch of sympathy for Michelle. "What about your whammy?"

"It didn't work. I must have done something wrong. I don't understand it. I didn't want yours to work, and it did. Hers I wanted to work, and it didn't. I guess I do everything wrong. I'm not surprised you don't want me for a friend."

"I never said that. But you could have told me about

your father and Diana. I would have understood something like that."

Michelle said meekly, "I really hate myself. But we had so much to talk about—Hugo and me. And so many plans to make. I mean, like what kind of strategy we'd use. When something like this happens, you just gotta line up your strategy right away. And then, I didn't think I should burden you with my problems."

"Oh, Michelle—" Amy gave a mildly disapproving shake of her head. "What are friends for?"

"You mean you wouldn't have minded if I burdened you?"

"What kind of a friend would I be if I minded that?" In her head, Amy had been accusing Michelle of disloyalty, and all the time Michelle and Hugo were only sharing a devastating problem—their father's coming marriage. Amy had suffered the same shattering experience. And she, too, had kept it to herself. Not because she was afraid of burdening her friends, but because she felt ashamed—as if it were all her fault, and if her friends found out, they would realize how ugly and worthless she was. How could she hold against Michelle something she had done herself? She said now, "I think I understand how you felt."

Michelle said quickly, "Does that mean you forgive me?"

What could Amy say except, "There isn't anything to forgive."

"Oh, yes, there is. Sometimes I am the meanest, rottenest person alive."

"Oh, no, you're not."

"Oh, yes, I am."

"Well, I don't think so."

"You don't?"

"No, I don't."

"Oh, I'm so glad to hear you say that. I was afraid you'd never forgive me. And I want you to know I'm going to make up for what I did to the doll. My dad will help me find a doll hospital, and I'll get it fixed."

"You don't have to do that."

"Yes, I do. I'd never forgive myself if I didn't."

"Well, if you really feel like that—"

"Oh, I do," Michelle said. Then she stared at Amy, her eyes clouding again. Finally she said, "Say you forgive me." Tears started to trickle down her cheeks.

Amy felt her own eyes fill up.

"Say it—please."

Michelle looked so miserable that Amy felt all choked up. "I forgive you if you forgive me." Now tears started running down Amy's cheeks, too.

Michelle sank down on the bed. The two put comforting arms around each other and both had a good cry. When they finished, they dried their eyes and swore everlasting friendship.

"Oh, I feel so much better," Michelle said.

"Me, too."

Then they both fell silent. After a long time, Michelle said, "Now I wish I could think of something funny to say."

"Me, too."

"I know—" A big grin spread over Michelle's face. "I got some rhinestones for the two of us—off an old evening bag my mother didn't want anymore. After school tomorrow, we'll buy some glue, and the next day we can wear them to school."

"On our foreheads, like the waitress in Farrell's?"

"Where else?"

They began to giggle over the thought of the great sensation they would create. Michelle said, "I'll go get them and show you."

It was only after she had gone that Amy thought of Hisa and the dollhouse. She realized with a pang that now there would be no dollhouse. Michelle would never have anything to do with a project like that, even if the other girls wanted her. If Amy went on with it and continued her friendship with Hisa, Michelle's feelings would be hurt. And not for anything would Amy hurt Michelle's feelings again.

Besides, Amy felt guilty about being so quick to misjudge Michelle's loyalty. The least Amy could do now was offer her own. After all, a best friend was more important than anybody. Or anything.

Amy sighed. She had so wanted to build that dollhouse.

Fifteen

Guilty, Guilty, Guilty!

WHEN THEY WORE the rhinestones to school, it was clear to everyone that Michelle was still a part of Amy's life. There was no further mention of building dollhouses. Although Amy regretted the loss of her new friends, the way they avoided Michelle seemed unfair to her. Their attitude made her feel more fiercely loyal than ever. With rhinestones placed brazenly in the middle of their foreheads, Amy and Michelle had, indeed, seemed like two against the world.

And when Michelle's father remarried, Amy couldn't have felt closer to her. She shared her grief and comforted her. Who but someone who had gone through the same thing herself could ease the pain of a friend?

But as the days passed, so did Amy's feelings of loyalty and of defiance, leaving in their place a kind of—she hated to admit it—resentment toward Michelle and, yes, even a touch of boredom with her. Nothing Amy wanted to do interested Michelle very much. And nothing Michelle wanted to do interested Amy very much. So they did what Michelle wanted to do. Amy couldn't help but feel that she was missing out on many things that were important to her. The worst part was that she had no idea of what to do about the situation.

Michelle kept her promise to have Aimee repaired. All alone one day she visited the antiques shop where they had seen the beautiful old doll with her performing bird. The woman who ran the shop told Michelle where she could take Amy's doll for mending. Now Aimee had a completely new body as well as a new dress. No one would ever know how she had suffered. Except Amy and Michelle.

Amy almost envied the doll. Sometimes she herself felt in need of repair. But she had no new parts she could exchange for the old to make everything all right again. The days drifted along and with them Amy, who was growing more and more resigned to the limitations her friendship with Michelle imposed upon her.

One day she and Michelle walked up to the village drugstore so that Michelle could have a prescription filled for her mother. On the way, Amy mentioned that her father had called the previous evening.

"Did you talk to him?" Michelle asked.

Amy said, "Of course not. You should know better than that."

"What did he want?"

"I don't really know. But my birthday's only a couple

of weeks away. I imagine it had something to do with that."

"Aren't you ever going to talk to him?"

"Never," Amy said.

"I don't blame you. Sometimes I think I should stop talking to my dad, too. Believe me, I don't say any more to Diana than I have to."

In that glum mood they entered the store. There were no other customers, so Michelle immediately handed the druggist her mother's prescription. He said it would take a few minutes and disappeared into a backroom.

While Michelle was admiring a jewelry display which the druggist had been setting up at the counter, Amy made for the open candy counter. She found some sugarless gum she liked, helped herself to a package, and took it back to join Michelle. As they waited, Amy noticed that what she had thought was a jewelry display was a small rack of pierced earrings. Another time, she might have nagged Michelle to join her in getting their ears pierced. But today the thought held no appeal for her.

The druggist finally returned with the prescription. Michelle paid him and Amy paid for her gum. Because the day was chilly, Amy was wearing a warm wool car coat with big patch pockets. She dropped the package of gum into a pocket as they left the store.

Outside, Amy paused for a moment in front of a window with a cosmetic display and glanced at a chart of lipstick shades.

"Oh, hurry," Michelle said shortly and kept walking.

Amy looked up, annoyed. "What's the rush?"

"I—I gotta go."

"Oh." Amy hurried and overtook Michelle. As they started up the street, a man's voice boomed behind them, "Just a minute, you kids!"

Michelle whirled around, almost knocking Amy over in the process. Quickly, she grabbed Amy, apparently to keep her from falling. In the next moment, someone snatched Amy's coat collar. Before she realized what was happening, the druggist was roughly yanking her and Michelle back into the store.

Once inside, he released them and said, "Okay, which one of you took it?"

Michelle, her voice shaky, said, "We don't know what you're talking about."

"Oh, you don't? This isn't the first time I've missed something after you kids have been in here. Now, do you want to turn it over or do you want the police to search you?"

At the mention of police, Amy's heart started pumping fast. The man must be crazy.

"I didn't take anything," Michelle said. "I paid you for the medicine."

"And I paid for the gum," Amy said. She reached into her pocket for it. Her hand closed over something hard. Instead of gum, she drew out an earring, a delicate hoop covered with seed pearls. She held it up and stared at it, bewildered.

"Where's the other one?" the druggist said.

She glanced up at him, confused. "What?"

"The other one."

Once more Amy reached into the pocket. This time she pulled out the gum and a second earring.

The druggist took both earrings from her. Then he said to Michelle, "You can go." He pointed to Amy. "This one stays."

It had taken Amy a moment to sort out things in her head. Now all was becoming clear, everything was falling into place. She looked at Michelle, expecting her to come to the rescue. Instead, Michelle shrank away and kept backing toward the door.

"Michelle?" Amy said, not quite believing her eyes.

Michelle, looking stricken, stared at Amy for a second. She opened her mouth as if to say something, closed it again, turned, and—with a fist doubled against her lips—fled from the store.

"I could have sworn she was the one," the druggist mumbled, but Amy paid no attention. All she could see was the box of earrings tumbling down in Michelle's closet. All of them stolen, she was certain now. She thought of the day in The Sorcerer's Den when she had frightened Michelle. Had she almost caught her in the act then?

She realized now that Michelle had not bumped her so hard accidentally when the druggist yelled at them. She must have used that moment to dump the earrings into

Amy's big pocket. Michelle, a thief. But why? The earrings weren't very expensive. And Michelle always had plenty of money. She could just as easily have bought them. Besides, unless she got her ears pierced, Michelle couldn't use the earrings anyhow.

"Okay," the druggist said. "What's your name? Where do you live?"

Amy wanted to shout that she had never in her life stolen anything. She started to say so, then for the first time realized the hopelessness of her situation. Who would ever believe her? She said dully, "My name is Amy Warner."

Sixteen

Pandora's Box

WHEN SHE SET off for school the following morning, Amy deliberately avoided the Mudds' apartment. She knew she would have to face Michelle soon, but she dreaded the encounter and was trying to postpone it. As it turned out, Michelle had apparently anticipated her thinking. When Amy stepped out of the elevator and into the lobby, Michelle was waiting for her.

"Hi," Michelle said, looking anxious.

"Hi," Amy said, her expression sober.

"I was going to call you last night. Then we all decided to go out to dinner, and we just got back too late." When Amy failed to respond, Michelle added, "I was early this morning. I thought I'd wait for you down here. You ready to leave?"

Just as if nothing had happened! "I'm ready to leave, but not with you."

Michelle was the picture of innocence. "Why not?"

"You know why not. Because I could have gone to jail for what *you* did."

Now little worried furrows began forming on Michelle's forehead. Abandoning her innocent pose, she asked, "What did he do to you?" She sounded almost afraid to find out.

Amy sighed. "He just talked to me—about what a serious crime stealing is and about how he wasn't going to do anything like tell anybody this time. He said I was young, and he wanted to give me a chance to change my ways. But if anything like that ever happened again in his store—" She broke off, still upset by the memory.

"That's all he did?" Michelle seemed as relieved as if she had been imagining herself in Amy's spot. As well she should!

Amy shook her head sadly. "How could you let me take the blame for your stealing?"

"Stealing? What stealing?"

"You stole those earrings, Michelle. When you thought you were going to get caught, you stuck them in my pocket."

Michelle said indignantly, "Oh, you are so wrong. I never stole any earrings. I was going to pay for them."

"When?"

"Well, later. All the money I had with me was what my mother gave me for the medicine. I was going to go home, get more money, go back, and pay him. And I didn't put them in your pocket. When you bumped into me, I dropped them. I couldn't help it if they fell where they did."

Even if Michelle's story had not had all kinds of holes, Amy would never have believed her. "What do you want them for anyhow? They're for pierced ears."

"What do I want them for?" Michelle took a second to answer. "What would anybody want something like that for? For when I get my ears pierced, of course. You know, when you get your ears pierced, you've gotta have a pair ready to stick in the holes right away."

"But you must have fifty pairs," Amy exclaimed.

Michelle's eyes narrowed. "What do you mean?"

Amy told her how she had come upon the box of earrings in the closet.

"I paid for those," Michelle said defensively. "You can't prove I didn't."

"I wasn't going to try to prove anything. The thing I don't understand is why you want all those earrings."

Michelle went into a long explanation of how she really adored earrings, was just dying to get her ears pierced, but her mother absolutely refused to let her.

When she finished, Amy said, "I don't believe you, Michelle. Once I would have, but not after yesterday."

Michelle's face took on a hurt expression. "If you were a true friend, you'd believe me."

Now came the hard part. Amy steeled herself. "That's what I have to tell you. I can't be your friend anymore."

Michelle's eyes widened in a look of disbelief. "But

you swore. We both swore we'd be friends forever."

Amy bit her lip. "I know I did. But I have to take it back. I just can't be your friend anymore." "Can't be" almost sounded as if she had some choice, as if tomorrow she could change her mind. The truth was, it was all over forever. It had something to do with the way you felt inside about somebody. Amy knew she could never again feel the same way about Michelle. It wasn't only that Michelle stole or even that she was willing and ready to make a victim of Amy. It had even more to do with something Amy's great-grandmother had believed. Friends, she said, were people you enjoyed, not people you needed. Along with all the other reasons, Amy no longer enjoyed Michelle.

Amy said, "I've got to go now. I don't want to be late for school." She hesitated a moment and then, in a voice that quivered a little, said, "Good-bye, Michelle," and turned away. Without another word, Amy hurried out the door as Michelle stood there staring at her.

For the rest of the day, Amy was plagued with feelings of guilt. She wondered if deep inside she wasn't glad of the excuse—any excuse, even this one—to break off with Michelle. She knew that the friendship was all over and that it was all for the best. Yet she couldn't help feeling wrong because she felt relieved.

The fact that Michelle was in the same class made things worse. Although Amy tried to avoid looking, once in a while, out of pure habit, she would glance over to find Michelle staring at her with a lost look. Amy refused to allow herself to feel even a tinge of sympathy. The friendship was over and nothing could revive it.

At lunchtime, Amy made a concerted effort to seek out Hisa and ask how the dollhouse was coming along.

Hisa acted guarded. "I've almost finished one room," she said, her voice polite but cool.

Amy was about to say something like, bet it looks nice, hoping that Hisa would pick up on the words and invite Amy to see her work. No, Amy decided. This was a matter of life and death. She would have to be direct and risk embarrassment. If she didn't immediately involve herself with other friends, Michelle might somehow manage to get back into her life. So she said, "Can I come over after school and see what you're doing?"

Hisa considered the matter. Finally, she said, "I thought you were too busy with Michelle to bother with something like a dollhouse."

Hoping she would understand, Amy said, "When Michelle and I were friends, she didn't like things like that. I guess I always felt I had to do what *she* wanted to do. That's why I didn't go on with the dollhouse."

"It sounds like you're not friends anymore."

"We're not."

"Oh." Hisa looked curious but, to Amy's relief, she didn't ask any questions. Instead, as if it were her own idea, she said, "Why don't you come over after school? We can walk home together."

133

Although she would never have dreamed of telling Hisa why, Amy felt deeply grateful.

A few days later Amy was caught up in the creation of the first room of her dollhouse. She was spending a part of each afternoon in Hisa's project room, working on a salon that would do justice to Mimi. It had to be very elegant, very regal, and very last-century. Amy was so busy that she gave almost no thought to Michelle.

This particular afternoon her mother had given her permission to stay at Hisa's nearly until dinnertime. When Amy arrived home, she found a large box propped against the apartment door. It was crudely wrapped in brown paper and addressed to her.

At first Amy thought that it was a birthday present from her father. Although the box was heavy and awkward, she managed to lift it and carry it inside with her.

At the click of the front door, the sound of her mother's typewriter died. "Is that you, Amy?" her mother called.

"Yes, it's me."

"I'll start dinner in a minute, honey. I just want to finish the page I'm working on."

"Okay." Amy took the box back to her bedroom, set it on the bed, and stared at it. She felt as disturbed as she'd felt with the arrival of Aimee. Finally she decided she'd better open the package and get her emotions in hand before she showed the gift to her mother. Only as she worked off the string did she realize that the box had not come through the mail. Neither stamps nor a return address were on it. In addition, the wrapping was so poorly done that it might have been the work of a child.

Feeling apprehensive now, she ripped off the paper, reached for the lid, then hesitated. Something came over Amy, almost a presentiment of something bad. When she finally lifted the lid, she did it as gingerly as if she expected Pandora's evils to rush out and inundate the world. Instead, she found herself staring at the old doll with the performing bird, the same doll she had last seen in the antiques shop she had visited with Michelle. The width of the box had even accommodated the birdcage.

Then she noticed the card. She picked it up to find a cat that looked very much like Mousy Tongue winking at her. Inside it read, "Have a Purr-fect Birthday." There was no signature.

Amy's throat went dry. In a moment, her eyes began to fill. She knew exactly what Michelle was trying to do, and the thought broke her up. Her birthday was still a couple of weeks away. Michelle had used that as an excuse to give her something so fabulous that Amy would never be able to resist accepting it. Silly Michelle. That was all the more reason why Amy would have to refuse it.

Even if she could accept a gift that valuable—which she could not—it would change nothing between her and Michelle. And the gift *was* valuable. Amy knew enough about the value of old dolls to hazard a guess. Michelle must have somehow drawn on the college fund her father had set up for her.

Then an icy fear gripped Amy. The woman who owned the antiques shop had said the doll was not for sale. No, Amy told herself, I must be wrong. As far as I know, Michelle has never stolen anything but earrings.

Amy hated herself for doing it, but she went out to the small service area where her mother piled newspapers until she threw them out. Amy went through all the local papers for four days back. To her relief, she found nothing.

Only when she passed the breakfast bar in the kitchen did she realize that she had missed the current day's paper. There it sat, unopened. She picked it up, removed the elastic band, and unfolded it. And there, almost exactly as she had imagined it, was a small article with a photograph of the old doll. She felt sick as she read the headline: "Valuable Antique Stolen from Local Shop."

From her television viewing, phrases like "receiver of stolen property" and "accessory after the fact" ran through her head. Now she was frightened. Really frightened. She could hear the druggist saying, "I gave her a chance when I should have turned her in. They start small, and the next thing you know they're robbing antiques and from there—who knows?—gas stations, maybe, even banks." Amy shuddered.

She picked up the paper and stared at it for a long time, while biting on the knuckle of her thumb. Finally she made her decision. She headed for her mother's room and stood in the doorway. When her mother glanced up from her typewriter, Amy swallowed hard and said, "Mom, can we talk? It's awfully important."

Seventeen
Money Well Spent

It was a Saturday. It was also the day that Michelle was moving to her father's apartment in Beverly Hills, about twenty-five miles away. Amy had spent the morning at Hisa's and planned to return in the afternoon when Barbara and Janie would join them. As she came home for lunch, she noticed Michelle's father's car parked out front.

Almost two weeks had gone by since Amy, feeling like a traitor, had tearfully told her mother about the thefts. Her mother had comforted her and said, "You did the right thing, Amy. It's important that Michelle's parents know. She could have gone on this way for years with no one doing anything for her. Now she'll have a chance to get the help she needs."

All too often Amy had accused her mother of not taking the time to talk to her. Now she felt a little unfair. When it really mattered her mother was not only willing to talk but to listen. And there was no question of her believing Amy. Mom did. She always did.

"But why does Michelle do it?" Amy had asked. "Why does she steal things she could pay for, things she can't use anyhow?"

"I suspect she's sick, Amy."

"But stealing isn't a sickness."

"Sometimes it is. I've read about people who can't control an urge to take some stupid little thing they could well afford to pay for. It's a strange kind of mental aberration. Perhaps Michelle is like that. At any rate, her parents simply have to know."

That was when her mother had called Mrs. Mudd and asked her to come over immediately, insisting it was urgent. When she arrived, Amy's mother took her into the living room and they talked. Although Amy kept to her room, the apartment was small enough for her to hear Mrs. Mudd when her voice rose somewhat hysterically. "I've always known that kid would get into some kind of trouble. I've had nothing but problems with her. Hugo now—" She went on for some time asking why Michelle couldn't be more like her brother.

When Amy's mother had calmed her down, Mrs. Mudd sent for Michelle's father. It took him almost an hour to get there. When he did, he talked to Michelle's mother, to Amy's mother, to Amy, and, later, in his former wife's apartment, to Michelle. Then he came back to talk again with Amy's mother and to pick up the stolen doll, which he planned to return immediately.

After Dr. Mudd left, her mother told Amy that he'd said Michelle had readily admitted her guilt to him.

"I feel terrible about telling on her." Amy wasn't quite sure of what she had set into motion.

"You mustn't feel guilty, Amy. There was nothing else you could have done. Now her father is going to see that Michelle gets help."

"She won't have to go to jail or juvenile hall or something?"

"Of course not. Not at her age. And not for this kind of thing."

"That's what I don't understand. What's this kind of thing?"

"Her father feels as I do that Michelle must be sick, that she's one of those people I told you about—people with a compulsion to steal. They can't really help themselves. They take things—silly things that they can't even use. In Michelle's case, earrings."

"But why?"

"According to her father, it could be for one of a number of reasons. Michelle might even be trying to take revenge against her mother because her mother favors Hugo."

"I don't understand," Amy said.

"Well, it's all very complicated. It's as if Michelle were saying to her mother, 'You make me feel worthless, so I might as well *be* worthless.' Something like that."

"I still don't understand."

"I can't say that I do either, really. But the important thing is Michelle is not a criminal. She's sick. That's all you and I have to understand. I'm sure Michelle doesn't understand herself why she does these things. Or why she steals only earrings for pierced ears."

Now Amy remembered something. "Her mother has pierced ears."

"Well, perhaps that has something to do with it. Perhaps the earrings, to Michelle, subconsciously symbolize something about her mother. Or they could even symbolize the love Michelle wants from her mother but feels she isn't getting. I don't know. And I'm no doctor, so I'm not going to make any more guesses."

"What about the doll? That didn't have anything to do with her mother. Why would she take something I was bound to find out was stolen?"

"Her father feels that was her cry for help. She wanted to be caught and punished for her deeds."

Amy couldn't really understand any of it. She only hoped that her mother was right about Michelle's wanting someone to catch her. Then perhaps Michelle wouldn't hate Amy so much for her part in the mess and for what had happened after. Michelle had already spent more than a week with her father and Diana. Now she was going to live with them for good.

To Amy's dismay, as she entered the lobby, Michelle and her father, both loaded down with luggage, stepped out of the elevator. Amy felt sure that Michelle, whom she hadn't seen since before the doll episode, would snub her. To Amy's surprise, Michelle set down the bag she was carrying and said, "I'll only be a minute, Dad. I want to say good-bye to Amy."

He nodded at Amy and continued toward the car.

"Hi," Michelle said.

"Hi," Amy said. The two stood staring at each other for a moment. Finally Amy said, "I'm sorry you're going to live with your father. I mean, I'm sorry on account of your stepmother."

"Diana?" Michelle shrugged. "She's not so bad."

"Oh? I'm glad."

"Yeah. In fact, she's a pretty good guy. Knows a lot of show-biz people. Big names, too. Has them over to the apartment all the time. You wouldn't believe how funny show-biz people are—I mean, witty-funny. It's really a riot at the apartment—just like a show. I've gotten so I hate to be away from the place—afraid I might miss something, y'know?"

"I'm glad," Amy said. "I mean, that it's a riot. I mean—well, I'm glad you like it."

"Yeah."

An uncomfortable silence fell. Michelle picked up her bag and shifted it from one hand to the other. At length she said, "You know, I've got my own shrink now."

"Oh?"

"Yeah. Of course I don't really need a shrink. I'm just preparing for my career."

"Oh?"

"Yeah. You see, before you can be a psychiatrist,

you've got to be psyched. I figure I'll get that part over with now."

"Oh."

Michelle shifted the bag again, then said, "Well, I guess I won't be seeing you. Not for a long time anyhow."

"Won't you be coming back to see your mother and Hugo?"

"Not if I go to school in Europe."

"You're going to school in Europe?"

"I might. I've been seriously thinking about it."

"Oh," Amy said. What else could she say? She didn't really believe Michelle would ever go to school in Europe.

There was another uncomfortable silence. Then Michelle said again, "Well, I guess I won't be seeing you." She made a feeble attempt at a grin. With a touch of bravado, she added, "You might say we're being divorced."

Amy tried her best to smile, but she could feel her lip tremble.

"Bye," Michelle said.

"Bye," Amy said. For a moment she almost thought Michelle was going to cry. Then Michelle turned and hurried after her father.

Amy went over to the elevator, pushed the button, and waited, a great lump in her throat. When the doors opened, Mousy Tongue appeared from someplace and dashed inside with her. As she looked down at him, the lump grew bigger. Tears began to well up in her eyes.

Even the cat's funny name reminded her of the first time she had met Michelle. How much they had shared since then, good and bad. Now she preferred to remember the good—good jokes, good stories, good times. It was important to remember the good. If you remembered the good, then, as her mother had once said, it was like money well spent.

By the time she entered the apartment, her eyes were dry again. Deep inside, she knew that she was better off without Michelle. And she even suspected Michelle was better off without her. Like a divorce?

When Amy went into the kitchen, her mother was fixing sandwiches for their lunch. "Your father called," she said.

"Oh?"

"Amy, he's going to call on your birthday. I think you should speak to him."

Amy opened her mouth to say no, then thought better of it. She found herself wondering if her mother and father's situation could have been anything like hers and Michelle's.

Her mother said again, "I really think you should speak to him, Amy."

Amy took another moment to consider, then said, "I'll think about it."

"Good."

"Now, I'm not saying I will, understand. I'm only saying I'll think about it."

Amy turned quickly away and went into her bedroom. She knew she had a big decision to make. And soon. Tomorrow was her birthday.